Supposing a deputation of excessively nice and polite mice appeared at the foot of the bed and said they wanted to thank you for saving their youngest member, and then told you they were in danger of starvation and death from fearful traps, and that it was all the fault of your aunt, wouldn't you want to help? Well, Fred certainly did – even though he had a feverish cold – and, with the help of his cousins and a sympathetic cat, Puss, he did.

He invited them to go and live in the Snow House, made from an enormous snowball which, with its tiny doors and windows and even a front gate, was just the right size for mice. There were difficulties, of course, night was fraught with peril, especially when the unruly element broke ranks and there was a deadly battle between Puss and Bouncer, the odious pug. But, eventually, the mice were all safely installed and happily living off the cakes and buns the children brought them, until something terrible happened – the mice were kidnapped, and seemed destined for a fate worse than death.

How Fred, Alice, Willie and Ben and Singleton, the smallest mouse, managed one of the biggest and most daring rescues in mouse history makes a marvellous finish to what seems to us a very special book indeed. Written by a new Puffin author who actually built the Snow House as a child and had some, if not all of Fred's adventures, it will be enjoyed by everyone who feels friendly towards mice. For reading aloud and privately from age seven to eleven.

Nora Wilkinson

The Snow House

Illustrated by Martin J. Cottam

Puffin Books

Puffin Books,
Penguin Books Ltd, Harmondsworth,
Middlesex, England
Penguin Books, 625 Madison Avenue,
New York, New York 10022, U.S.A.
Penguin Books Australia Ltd, Ringwood,
Victoria, Australia
Penguin Books Canada Ltd, 2801 John Street,
Markham, Ontario, Canada L3R 1B4
Penguin Books (N.Z.) Ltd, 182–190 Wairau Road,
Auckland 10, New Zealand

First published by Kestrel Books 1980
Published in Puffin Books 1981

Made and printed in Great Britain by
Richard Clay (The Chaucer Press) Ltd, Bungay, Suffolk
Set in Linotype Juliana

1

Young Fred stared through the bedroom window at the falling snow. It had started to snow at the beginning of December, and it had gone on snowing, day after day, until Fred had quite forgotten what the streets looked like before they were white and frozen. Indeed, he was not sure sometimes which was outdoors and which was indoors. The whiteness of the world mesmerized him. When he played outside with his cousins the snow was crusty and dry. It was reflected in the shop windows, and at night it was illuminated and coloured by the lights inside the shops. The green and red flasks in the chemist's spilt their dyes into the street, and twisted shapes of the jars and biscuit tins in his own father's shop window were flung by the bottle-glass panes in dark patches on to the snow. It was all shadows and lights, and the reflections came back again on to the walls inside.

'It can't get any colder,' Alice had said, blowing into her woollen gloves to warm her red fingers.

But it did. Alice and Willie and young Fred skated up and down all through the Christmas holidays. Little Benjamin, who was only three, slid along after them, holding on to Alice's skirt, and the children's breath smoked in great puffs about their faces. Now there was only one day left before they had to go back to school, and young Fred, staring through the window, wondered if Aunt Jen would let him go out to play, or if she would fuss about his wet clothes.

Fred sighed. He wished Mam would come home. As he

watched the snowflakes drifting idly past the window he remembered the day that now seemed so long ago, when his mother had gone away. It must have been early in November, before the snow began. Fred had come in late from a bonfire party in the Square, his cheeks rosy with excitement and the heat of the fire, and the stars of the fireworks still dancing in his eyes. He pushed open the door, clicking the latch with a clumsy impatient thumb, and found the doctor in the kitchen talking solemnly to his father.

'It can't be helped, man,' the doctor was saying. 'She's in quite a bad way, you know. The sanatorium's the only place.'

Nobody seemed to notice Fred. When his father raised his face it was grey, and there was fear in his eyes. He looked at the doctor, and said, very slowly, 'What's the prospect, then?'

The doctor waved his spectacles in the air and clapped Dad on the shoulder. 'Now Fred,' he said, 'there's no question at all. She'll get better, I promise you, but it will take time. We just caught it. Good thing you called me. And here's the boy –' He turned to smile at young Fred who was standing bewildered in the doorway. 'He'll need to be taken care of. Can you get some help? How were the fireworks, lad?'

Young Fred opened his mouth, but did not know what to say. There was an uncomfortable feeling in the kitchen. His mother's work-basket lay on the floor beside her chair, his own socks trailing over the edge, one of them half darned with a wooden mushroom in the heel and a darning needle sticking out of it. He looked at her empty chair, at the doctor's cheerful face, and at his father's anxious eyes.

'Where's Mam?' he said.

He could not remember very clearly what had happened during the next few days. A carriage had come and his mother had gone away in it. Her cough had got worse, Dad explained, and she had to go to hospital to get better. Aunt Jen was coming to look after them until Mam was well enough to come home again. And so Aunt Jen had arrived, and soon after that the snow had started – and home, for Fred, became a very different place.

The house where Fred lived was part of a double-fronted shop that stood in one of the wide back streets of a small West Yorkshire town. Fred's father was a grocer and dry goodsman, and the shop had not changed in appearance since his own father had kept it. Its full name was The Sundial Stores, but everybody just called it The Sundial. There were two bow-fronted windows, and the door, with its tiny, tinkling iron bell, stood in between. The old sundial from which the shop got its name was on the wall above the door. It told true time, summer and winter, on sunny days. In one window there were groceries, and in the other, wines and spirits in bottles and small casks and great stone jars. Children used to play at looking in through the shop windows with their noses pressed flat against the bottle-glass, to make the tins of rice and tea and demerara sugar shiver and twist their shapes.

Aunt Jen did not at all like The Sundial as a home. 'Like living in a warehouse,' she said, with a disapproving sniff.

And, indeed, that is exactly what it had been before Fred's grandfather bought it and converted it into a shop in front and a house behind. That was years ago, before Dad was even born; but the house still seemed to grow casually out of the shop and everywhere, upstairs and downstairs, the smells of soap and sugar and coffee and spices lingered. Before Mam went away it had all been warm and comfortably untidy. It was full of surprises, and Fred loved it. The back door was on the street corner and it opened directly into the kitchen in which everybody lived. In the kitchen there were the 'catsteps' – a thick oak plank fixed flat against the wall, to make a ladder. It was a relic of the old

warehouse, and led up into what had once been a storeroom but was now the bathroom above the kitchen. It was no ordinary ladder. The wood was polished and grained and shiny, with elliptical footholds and handholds set alternately left and right all the way up to the top.

'Dangerous thing,' said Aunt Jen, and never climbed it. She used the ordinary staircase behind the kitchen, but Fred went up and down the catsteps, and so did his cousins, leaving, to Aunt Jen's annoyance, muddy footprints on the bathroom floor.

The bathroom was large and lofty. The lino on the floor was shiny and slippery and chilled Fred's bare feet. The bath was enormous, set in a kind of mahogany coffin, and it had an extraordinary metal plunger which had to be wrenched up to let the water out. The water ran away with a dreadful sound, like a giant hiccupping. From the bathroom another little ladder, steep and shaky, led still higher into the loft, where Puss habitually kept her kittens. The loft, and the cellars that ran under the whole length of the house and the shop, were the only places left undisturbed by Aunt Jen's compulsive cleaning. The cellars, three underground rooms leading from one to another, were dark and cold and mysterious, with stone shelves full of dusty bottles, mouldy boxes and cobwebby jars. They were inhabited, Aunt Jen was convinced, by millions of mice.

She hated mice. 'Nasty dirty things,' she said, 'running all over the place.' But Fred was used to them. When he went down the stone steps into the cellar, carrying a paraffin lantern that made the shadows jump and dance, he was accustomed to hearing a rustling and a pattering, a perpetual faint stirring and settling, like a sigh. And Mam had always regarded the mice with her usual easy-going tolerance.

'They don't do any harm,' she said, 'and they clear up the crumbs.'

But there were no crumbs any more, young Fred thought

sadly, since Aunt Jen had come to The Sundial. He did not care for Aunt Jen. She was thin and spidery, and her waist-bands were very tight, and she was always worrying about things like wet socks and clean handkerchiefs. And cobwebs. And mice. She swept and scrubbed and polished and cooked, and never seemed to have time to laugh or play. When she put Fred to bed she gave him an anxious peck on his cheek, and tucked in the bedclothes as if she were tying up a parcel. His mother always used to say, ''Night, young Fred,' with her mouth against his ear and her fingers ruffling his hair. Aunt Jen, as she went out of the bedroom, just sniffed.

There was a sudden joyful shouting down below in the street, as Fred's cousins came sliding and dancing round the corner. Alice's eyes were sparkling, and the dark hair that drifted below her woollen cap was flecked with snowflakes.

'Come on out,' shouted Willie. 'We're making a giant snowball.'

'You'll have to help us,' Alice called. 'It's getting too big and heavy.'

'Come on, Fred, come on,' echoed Benjamin, and as he waved his arms he lost his balance and sat down with a bump in the snow. Alice dragged him to his feet and brushed him down, while Fred raced down to the kitchen to fetch his coat, and Willie came bursting in through the door, breathless with impatience. Fred snatched his cap from the peg and struggled into the sleeves of his coat. Aunt Jen, who was peeling onions, looked at him anxiously over her spectacles, rubbing away the tears that were beginning to trickle from her smarting eyes.

'Fasten up your coat, boy,' she said. 'And you'll want your scarf ... I don't know that you ought ...' but before she could say any more to stop him, Fred and Willie had dashed out of the house, and the door slammed behind them.

2

Alice and Ben had already disappeared round the corner.
The boys raced and slithered after them, and in the little
Square where Uncle John's bakehouse stood, and where
Fred's cousins lived, they came to the snowball and began
to roll it round. They rolled it and rolled it until it was
bigger than any of them. It was a magnificent snowball,
huge and hard and icy and heavy. They heaved and pushed
and still it grew, bigger and bigger, until at last it was too
heavy to push any more. The children were out of breath
and exhausted, with aching arms and frozen fingers.

'It's bigger than the world,' said Benjamin, staring up at
it. 'Can I sit on it?' Willie and Fred tried to lift him on to
the snowball, but it was too high and too slippery.

'We can't make it any bigger,' Alice said sadly. 'It's too
heavy to move.'

Then Willie began to scoop up handfuls of snow and
pack them on to the snowball. They all joined in, and went
on building it up until not even Alice, who was the tallest
of them, could reach the top. They stood back and gazed
at it, and Benjamin stumbled off towards the bakehouse,
shouting, 'Dad! Dad! Look, Dad!'

Uncle John was one of the best people in young Fred's
world. There he was, standing in the doorway at the top of
the Square, laughing at the children's games. Then all at
once, while Benjamin trotted towards him, he came flying
out of the bakehouse with his apron dancing and frost on
his whiskers, like a giant; a great knife in one hand and a
cleaver in the other. With these weapons he made an on-
slaught on the snowball, laughing all the time, and the
laughter smoked out of his mouth in the frosty air. Within

a few minutes he had carved the snowball into a house fit for a lord, at such a speed that the children did not perceive the supreme craft he brought to his work. Before their wondering eyes he cut out windows and doorways. With enormous energy he scraped out the heart of the snowball so that it became a hollow shell, a round house, a real dwelling place. He made a snow gate, and a row of railings, with a carriage-drive leading up to the front door. Chimneys grew out of the roof, and white hedgerows round the back of the house; and it was all fashioned out of ice and frozen snow.

The children were spellbound. Little Ben blew through the windows of the snow house. 'But who will live in it?' he said. 'I can't get in.'

'You're too big a lad,' said Alice, rubbing his head in an ecstasy of happiness, as she gazed at the shining miracle. 'It's just about right for mice, though, I reckon. It's lovely, Dad. It's like a Christmas cake.'

'Don't you try eating it, then,' said Uncle John, and went off back to the bakehouse on a great gust of laughter. He turned in the doorway and waved his carving knife at the children. 'You might get tenants for your snow house,' he called across the Square. 'Put up a notice – TO LET.' and he disappeared into the bakehouse. The rich warm smell of bread and pastries and pies drifted across the Square, as warm and rich as Uncle John's laughter.

Alice and Willie skipped and danced round the snow house, whooping like Indians. Benjamin poked his finger through the windows and doorways, and made his two red mittens trot up and down the carriage drive like little horses, shouting 'Gee up there! Gee up Dobbin!' But young Fred stood as still as a stone, his eyes swallowing the white beauty of the sparkling snow house, lost in a dream.

'If only I could be little enough,' he thought, 'I could live in it all by myself till Mam comes home, and Aunt Jen

12

would never know where I was. Puss could come too, and Alice could come for tea. But nobody else – nobody at all – never . . .'

'Come on,' said Ben, tugging at Fred's scarf. 'Come on home. It's cold.'

It was indeed very cold. Fred slowly followed his cousins across the Square to the bakehouse, looking back at the huge transfigured snowball. He was shivering, his teeth chattered, and his feet felt suddenly icy and heavy. There were mugs of hot sweet milk ready for the children, but when Auntie Patty looked at Fred's white face she raised her eyebrows. 'Bless you, child. You'd better come by the fire,' she said, as she drew off his gloves and began to rub his frozen fingers. 'Why didn't your uncle bring you in before? You're chilled through.' Young Fred sat down cross-legged on the rug by the fire, but he did not seem able to swallow his milk. He could not stop shivering and he felt very dizzy and queer. 'You look like a poor starved tailor,' said Auntie Patty. 'There's only one place for you, my lad. Take him home, Alice, do. Goodness knows what Aunt Jen is going to say.'

Alice took Fred's hand, and they walked back to The Sundial together, past the snow house which still sparkled and shone. Dinner at The Sundial – Aunt Jen's stew and rice pudding – was ready in the kitchen. Fred's father was sitting at the table, wearing his hat, as he always did. Alice said, 'Young Fred's not well.'

'Just look at that boy,' said Aunt Jen, accusing the world. 'Wet through with snow and as pale as a pikelet. You'd better change your clothes.'

The kitchen suddenly swam before Fred's eyes. He staggered towards the table, crying, 'Dad . . . Dad,' and tumbled to the floor at his father's feet.

The next thing that he really remembered was Aunt Jen's face looking anxiously down at him. He must have

been in bed quite a long time. It was dark, except for the reflection of the snow on his bedroom wall, and the pool of pale golden light from the candle on the chest of drawers. Aunt Jen had thrust a hot brick, wrapped in an old flannel nightshirt, into his bed, and she was standing beside him with a steaming cup of broth.

'Now drink this down, young Fred. It'll do you good.' And she began to spoon the broth with fierce concern into his mouth, grumbling all the time in muttered half-sentences. 'Whatever would your Mam say ... giving us all a fright ... wet through with snow ... what your uncle was thinking of ... chilled to the bone ... another one in hospital I shouldn't wonder ... do my best ... weak chests in the family ... doctor's coming tomorrow ... that's another thing ... nasty dirty things ... a trap down there tonight ... I'll get rid of them, that I will ... now drink it down ...' she grumbled on, putting a spoonful of warm broth into Fred's mouth.

Young Fred swallowed his broth dutifully and with difficulty. His throat was very swollen, his head was hot, and his mind confused. Aunt Jen tucked him into bed in the usual tight parcel, blew the candle out, and departed.

'I'll leave the door open,' she said. 'If you want anything, call out.'

She scurried downstairs, leaving him in the dark. As he drifted in and out of sleep, he vaguely remembered his father carrying him upstairs. He remembered the snow house and his cousins dancing round it. He heard the murmur of voices from Aunt Jen and his father who were talking downstairs. The voices seemed a long way off, coming and going, until at last the house was quiet. Everybody had gone to bed.

[3]

A faint grey light, made brighter by the snow-covered street, glimmered through the bedroom window. Young Fred turned over in bed and half-opened his eyes. 'It must be nearly morning,' he thought to himself. 'I wonder if it's still snowing.' He would have liked to look out of the window and see, but his bed was warm and comforting and the air round his nose was chilly. He stretched out his legs and touched the flannel-wrapped brick, which was still warm. He thought about the snow house shining like a jewel in the Square. He thought about Mam, and wondered if she would ever come home. He thought about Aunt Jen –

and suddenly he was sitting up, wide awake, with the sound of her voice ringing in his ears. 'Nasty dirty things ... I'll get rid of them ... putting a trap down tonight ... *putting a trap down* ... a T R A P.'

Young Fred had seen mouse traps in the corn chandler's. His own father, who sold most things, had never had such a thing in his shop. There was a dreadful click about the sound of the word that frightened Fred. He thought of the mice, whom he had often glimpsed scampering in the cellar amongst the bins and boxes. They were part of his life at The Sundial, and his heart turned over as he imagined them captured and helpless in the dark.

He climbed out of bed and groped about on the chest of drawers. Aunt Jen, thank goodness, had forgotten to take away the matches. Shivering in his nightshirt, as much from fear as from cold and fever, young Fred found the box and opened it with trembling fingers. The first match he struck went out in a sputter of flame. Steadying his hand, he struck another and lit the candle. The light grew into a golden spire. Fred listened for a moment, shielding the candle flame with his hand, by the open door. Anxiety and fear had given him an unfamiliar kind of cunning.

All was quiet in the house. He crept bare-footed out of his bedroom, and through the bathroom, and, holding the candlestick in one hand, he began to climb down the cat-steps into the kitchen. The glow of the kitchen fire was a red star to guide him, and its warmth comforted his bare legs as he made the careful descent. Softly he went across the kitchen floor. He opened the shop door, letting in the smells of oatmeal and raisins, coffee and peppermints, and crossed behind the counter to the cellar door. It creaked when he opened it, and young Fred held his breath. Nothing stirred in the rooms upstairs, and he continued his journey down the cold stone steps into the cellars. When he reached

16

the foot of the steps he stopped again and listened, holding the candle high.

A faint shriek, diminutive and full of despair, guided him across the cellar floor. He looked about, peering through the darkness. For a moment he could hear the familiar scampering of tiny feet, but as the candle moved, the sound died. He listened. From the far corner of the second cellar, by the flour bins, there came again that small despairing shriek. He tracked the sound and, stooping down between the bins, found its source. A mouse, beguiled by a lump of cheese, was imprisoned in a box with a treacherous door which had come clattering down to keep it waiting for tomorrow's death. It was a very small mouse.

Fred had no experience of trap mechanisms, and it was quite five minutes before he managed to release the catch and lift the door so that the tiny mouse could run free. He watched it go, then shut the trap, picked up his candle, and crept back, as quietly as he had come, to his bedroom. His feet were blue with cold, but his head felt hotter than ever. He blew out the candle, climbed painfully back into bed, and fell into a feverish sleep.

It was some time before he became aware of the voices. Very low voices, talking rapidly in a language he could not at first understand; a chorus of whispers, out of which, as he slowly emerged from sleep, occasional words seemed to come. He sat up in bed, rubbing his eyes, not sure if he were awake or dreaming. 'It must be morning. It must be tomorrow,' he thought. Then he saw that moonlight was flooding his bedroom with a white brilliance that made the shadows dark and deep. The snowlight made it brighter still, and in the brightness he could see a host of shining eyes and silvery whiskers. There were mice – at least twenty of them – sitting on his bed. Some were crouched on the chest of drawers, and more in the darker corners of the

17

room. One sat on the edge of the washbowl, watching him closely. Another, larger than the rest, perched on his pillow.

The low whispering stopped, and close to his ear Fred heard words that he could understand. The mouse on his pillow was actually talking to him. Young Fred stared at it in amazement.

'We are deeply obliged,' said the mouse with a courteous bow, 'not to say indebted. We would repay you, sir, but we are in grave peril ourselves. We come to express our humble gratitude.'

'Eh?' said Fred.

The mouse looked startled. A ripple of laughter went round the rest of the company, such quiet laughter that it sounded no more than the rustle of dry leaves.

Another mouse spoke. This time it was the one perched on the washbowl. 'He always talks like that,' it said. 'He's old fashioned and he can't get out of the habit. Fact is, you saved his great-great-grandson from a dreadful fate. It might have been any one of us, so we've all come along to say thanks. Also we're a bit scared, as you might say, and we're very glad to find a friend. One trap today, two perhaps tomorrow. We don't know at all where it's going to end.'

Young Fred looked round at his visitors. They were of various sizes and, he supposed, of various ages. The biggest mouse, who had first spoken with such grave courtesy, looked very old indeed. His whiskers were tipped with white, his fur was grizzled, and he seemed altogether venerable. At the foot of the bed five very small mice clustered together. Others, some brown, some grey, were sitting in small groups on the counterpane. He could not count how many there were on the floor, though he could see their bright round eyes gleaming in the shadows. Fred drew in his breath and tried to collect his wits.

'But if you know it's a trap,' he said, 'why do any of you have to get caught? Why can't you just keep away?'

The twittering and squeaking broke out again among the assembled mice. They all seemed to be talking at once, but Fred could not make out any words at all. Then the mouse on the washbowl spoke again. 'They can't all speak your language,' he explained. 'Some of the youngsters haven't learnt it yet, and some of the others, who should know better, haven't bothered.' He squeaked severely at a group of mice on the window-ledge, and they hung their heads and looked guilty. 'It's quite important,' the mouse went on, 'to know what you people are talking about. We need to know friend from foe. Forewarned is forearmed, and there'd be fewer accidents.'

There was a universal light sigh. A grey mouse spoke from the foot of the bed. 'It's cheese, you see. Once we smell cheese, we forget. We just go for it. We can't help ourselves.' Another very thin-faced mouse, crouching in the shadows, added, 'There isn't much, nowadays. There are the children to feed, and what with tins and wooden boxes and all the floor-cleaning that goes on now there's hardly a crumb left for us.' Fred had a vision of Aunt Jen on her knees scrubbing the kitchen floor till it glittered. A tired-looking elderly mouse took up the tale.

'Paper bags, paper bags. They were the thing. You could always get through a paper bag and have a dribble of oatmeal. But now it's all tins and bins and boxes. No hope at all.' The mouse brushed his whiskers sadly with his paws and settled down on the counterpane looking weary and disheartened.

The old mouse on Fred's pillow rose stiffly to his feet, and spoke with great dignity. 'Such cavilling and complaining is inappropriate,' he said. 'We have come here with a purpose, and we must shortly retire to take counsel for the future. The memories of mice, as my friend has said, are unfortunately very short. We not only forget dangers easily, but it is sometimes difficult for us to remember our allies.

But you have befriended us and saved a young life. We wish for a token to remember you by. We would humbly ask you, sir, to name this child.'

Fred felt the touch of a tiny claw on his hand, and recognized the little creature that had crept up and was crouching close to him as the baby mouse he had released from the trap. It looked rather fearfully up at him. Fred put out his finger and gently stroked its head. He looked round once more at the mice, who waited expectantly.

'But I don't know what names you like,' he said. 'My name's Fred and my cousins are Willie and Alice and Benjamin, and there's Uncle John and Auntie Patty, and Uncle Anthony and my Dad. He's called Fred, too. And ... and Aunt Jen. Would any of those names do?'

'They would sound a little strange to our ears,' said the old mouse, politely but rather dubiously, 'and would be untranslatable into our own language. A name with more significance, perhaps ... ?'

Young Fred was quite at a loss, and the mouse on the washbowl came to the rescue.

'It's like this,' he explained. 'Mice aren't given names until they come of age; that is, when they're a month old. This little chap is only a fortnight old yet, but it's a special occasion. He's called Thirteen, by the way, for the present, for obvious reasons. This ...' bowing deferentially towards the old mouse on the pillow, 'is our chief, Caradoc. We call him Sir. He's the oldest among us and comes of a noble and ancient family. My own name is Almond. When I was very young I had such a weakness for nuts that I used to go into your shop in broad daylight and steal them from the bag. I don't know how I escaped with my life. I was very foolish, and my name was given to me as a reminder and a warning. All our names mean something, you see. But most of us are called after the places our forefathers came from. We haven't always lived here, you know. We gathered here

20

from far and wide years ago, because it seemed a good place to live. And so it was, until recently. But now we are beginning to wonder.'

'Indeed. We are thinking seriously of moving on,' put in Caradoc, 'though the weather at present is highly inclement for journeys. But who knows what tomorrow may bring? Continue, Almond.'

'Sir,' said Almond. And turning back to Fred, he went on. 'This is Dewsbury' – pointing to the tired-looking mouse on the bed who had bemoaned the loss of paper bags. 'Over there, five brothers; Arthington, Eccup, Shadwell, Scarcroft and Follifoot. Their family used to live round about Harrogate. This little lot' – waving his paw towards the foot of the bed where seven small mice were sitting together – 'are due to be named tomorrow. They're Cleveland-Tontine's grandchildren; county people, they all used to be. They still think they're a cut above the rest of us, so I expect they'll have to be given double-barrelled names. Still, they're good sorts, and very reliable. My friend over there has exceptionally good eyes and seems to be able to see both ways at once. His name is Janus. Names have to tell you something, you see.' He paused for breath, and Caradoc stirred uneasily on Fred's pillow.

'Time presses,' he said. 'Pray make haste, Almond. Speak of the child.'

'Thirteen,' Almond went on. 'He's a singleton, you see. Very unusual amongst our people. We go in for large families. He has, as you may guess, twelve older brothers and sisters, but they are all grown up, and when Thirteen was born he was only the one. Only one instead of a litter. Very unusual indeed.' He paused again. Fred was puzzled.

'But what about his Mam and Dad?' he asked. 'Don't they want to choose his name? '

There was a moment's silence, and then Caradoc answered Fred's question. 'The child's mother and father are, alas, no longer with us. An accident befell them a few days after his birth. It is a miracle that he survived. Had it not been for Almond ...'

Almond looked down at his paws in some embarrassment, and spoke hastily. 'My wife and I ... well, we're looking after him with our own family until he comes of age. He's no trouble, as a rule, and he's the only one. Not like a whole extra litter to bring up. Besides, he's rather different.' He glanced at Caradoc, and then ran lightly across the bed and spoke quietly to the baby in the squeaky language that the other mice had used. Thirteen looked at Almond, and then up at Fred, and his eyes seemed to grow rounder than ever. Fred gathered up the tiny creature and cradled him carefully in his two hands. Thirteen blinked twice, shivered his whiskers, yawned, and fell suddenly asleep with his tail curled round his nose.

'A singleton,' said Fred softly, looking down at him. 'Like me. Couldn't you call him Singleton?'

There was an excited murmur from the mice. Caradoc looked down at the baby sleeping in Fred's protective hands. 'That is indeed a name full of meaning, and I am proud to bestow it. He shall be named before his time. We shall know him henceforth as Singleton.'

There was a solemn pause, as all the mice nodded their heads. Young Fred was partly awed by the dignity of Caradoc and partly seized with a great desire to laugh at the ponderous gravity of such very ordinary small animals. As he hovered between respect and amusement his dilemma was solved for him. Outside in the snowy street a door slammed, and heavy footsteps began to clatter on the frozen road. 'The wakeners-up!' cried Fred. 'It must be morning.'

There was a great scurry and a patter of feet. Mice leapt off the bed in alarm, scrambled down from the furniture and scampered away into the darkness, Janus leading the way.

Caradoc rose stiffly to his feet, bowed graciously to Fred, raised a paw in farewell, and vanished. Almond was the last to leave. He roused Thirteen from his sleep and, taking the little mouse with him, went towards the door. There he paused, and turned to say goodbye.

'Oh dear,' said Fred, 'where will you all go? Shall I never see you again? Won't you come back tomorrow?'

'Who knows what tomorrow may bring?' said Almond, repeating Caradoc's words. 'We should be sorry to leave. We have lived here a long time. But Caradoc will decide.' The last words ended in a squeak, and Fred was left alone.

He lay bemused. He heard the husky voices of the wakeners-up, and the tap-tap of their wire brushes on bedroom window panes. They came every morning, these white-headed old men, stamping through the dark, to waken the mill-workers and get them to work on time. Human alarm clocks, they earned a few pence a week for their services. 'Don't be late in the morning,' they cried again and again. 'Five o'clock by the Town Hall clock.' Slowly their calls grew fainter and fainter, and faded into the distance. Reality, and the chilly air, and the memory of a dream, beset Fred's thoughts. Was it a dream? He could not sort it out in the grey dawn. He shuffled down into the warmth of his bed, covered his head with the quilt, and fell asleep.

[4]

Young Fred woke late the next morning. The memories of the previous night's adventure crowded back into his mind, but seemed strange and unreal. Caradoc and Almond . . . did they really exist and had they really talked to him? He wasn't sure. He still felt light-headed. His throat was sore and his arms and legs were curiously heavy. He sat up in bed as Aunt Jen came into his bedroom, and greeted her with an enormous sneeze.

'A real chill, that's what you've got,' Aunt Jen announced with brisk satisfaction. 'No school for you today, boy. You'll stay in bed until the doctor comes.' She had brought a jug of hot water and gave his hands and face a brisk going-over with a flannel. 'There,' she said, 'you'll feel better now.' Oddly enough, Fred did. 'I'll bring you some porridge in a minute. Keep your strength up.'

Fred felt that his strength was being forced back into him by Aunt Jen's determination. He held the warm bowl of porridge with one hand against his chest, and between spoonfuls he said, 'Alice and Willie ... have they gone to school?'

'I should hope so,' said Aunt Jen. 'It's after ten o' clock. Now if you've finished you can lie down and have another sleep. The doctor will be coming before long.'

Fred relinquished his bowl and gratefully laid his head back on the pillow. 'Will Alice come and see me later on please?' he asked hopefully. And then as an afterthought: 'Thank you, Aunt Jen. That was nice.'

Aunt Jen's mouth suddenly quivered and she turned away. 'You've got to be a good boy now and stay quiet,' she said. 'Your Mam's my only sister and I promised her I'd see you right. Your Dad's coming up in a minute to see how you are. He came up last night but you were sound asleep. You wouldn't believe it ... cunning little things ... no cheese left in that trap but no sign of a mouse.'

Young Fred, who had for a moment felt a pang of conscience at Aunt Jen's unexpected show of feeling, now found his face growing scarlet when she spoke about the mousetrap. He tried to bury himself in his pillow, and Aunt Jen looked at him with a frown.

'You've got a temperature,' she muttered as she dived into the bottom of his bed to extract the brick in its flannel overcoat. 'When the doctor's been I'll go down to Jepson's and get some more mousetraps. Nasty dirty things ...' and clasping the brick under her arm she sniffed away downstairs with the empty porridge bowl.

So it was true, thought Fred, and he had not been dreaming. He lay thinking, his fingers idly playing with the edge of his blanket. 'I must save them somehow,' he said to himself. 'If there are going to be more traps ... Alice will help. I do hope Aunt Jen lets her come. But wherever can they go?'

He was still pondering on the problem half an hour later when his father came upstairs accompanied by Dr James. The doctor was an elderly man with gold-rimmed spectacles, which he put on and off repeatedly, using them more as an extension of his gestures than to see through. He talked very rapidly, and every time he stopped talking he peered closely at Fred like a bright inquisitive bird.

'What's all this about, then? What have you been playing at, young man? Let's have a listen to the band, eh?' He pulled up Fred's nightshirt and pressed the cold cup of his stethoscope against the boy's chest. 'Not the weather for chills and coughs. How long has he been like this, Fred?'

The words came tumbling out of his mouth like a rattle of marbles. He stared suddenly at Fred and then at his father, who said, 'Yesterday, just. Out in the snow with John's children. He came in frozen and then he ran a fever.'

Dr James prodded young Fred's ribs with his fingers and listened attentively to his chest. 'Full orchestra,' he said, rolling up his stethoscope. 'Fever, that's about right; but keep him warm, light diet, lots of drinks, and he should be all right in a few days. Nothing to worry about if you take care. He's got a touch of bronchitis. How's Annie, have you heard?'

'She writes every week,' said Dad, 'and doesn't complain. It's been a long time for young Fred. The trouble's clearing

25

up but we'll have to wait a while longer. She's allowed up, she says, every morning, and for an hour after tea. Maybe in the spring ...'

'No sense in rushing things. Takes time. You should be at school, young man, but you'll have to wait a few days. What's that ice-palace I saw in the Square, eh?' The doctor waved his spectacles at Fred and slammed them back on to his nose.

'It's our snow house,' said Fred. 'We made a snowball, Alice and Willie and me, and Uncle John made a house for us. Is it still there?'

'Still there? I should think it is,' said the doctor, snatching his spectacles off his nose again and twirling them round and round. 'Best house I've ever seen.' He pushed his face down close to Fred's. 'A snowball, you said? It's more like the universe. If this weather holds it will be there till Easter. Stay where you are, now. No going out to play in your snow house for a bit, eh? Leave it for a few days. It will still be waiting for you. No sign of a break in the weather, eh, Fred?' The doctor turned to young Fred's father with a grin and another wave of his spectacles. 'Keeps my surgery busy,' he said. 'I'll make up some medicine for this young chap.' And the two men, old friends, stumped off downstairs, talking together.

In a few minutes young Fred's father came back alone. He sat down at the bedside, pushed his hat down on to his head, and said, 'Well, young Fred?'

Young Fred traced the shape of a mouse on the back of his father's hand with his forefinger. 'Well, Dad,' he murmured in reply.

'What's on your mind?' said Dad.

There was a silence, during which Fred looked at his father and Dad looked back at Fred. Dad's face suddenly broke into a map of twinkling lines. 'Well?' he said, once more.

26

The words came tumbling out of young Fred's nervous mouth. 'It's the mice, Dad. Aunt Jen's setting traps in the cellar and they might all get caught, and Caradoc and Almond won't know what to do and there's a baby – Thirteen he's called, only his real name is Singleton – he's got no Mam and Dad and –'

'Whe-hey,' said his father, putting a brake on Fred's excitement which was bringing him near to tears. 'Like the doctor said, you *have* got a fever.' Fred looked helplessly at his father, trying to convince him. Dad looked back at Fred with a quizzical grin. 'Traps, did you say? Don't worry about that. I'll sort them out. After all, poor Aunt Jen, she shouldn't be going down the cellar steps in the dark. I'll take them down for her' – he gave a huge wink at young Fred – 'and I'll make sure they don't catch any mice.' He was suddenly serious, and looked for a moment very like Uncle John. 'We've had mice in the cellar since I was your age, young Fred, and they never did anybody any harm. Your Mam has always been fond of them. There's plenty for all, in this house. I'll see to it, never fret.'

Young Fred breathed heavily in his relief. But something told him it was only a temporary truce. His father felt obliged to Aunt Jen; and in any case Dad was absent-minded. He made promises, and meant to keep them; but as Fred knew from sad experience, he forgot. Still, Fred was grateful for this particular promise. He was sure the mice would be safe tonight.

His father was still looking at him with curious eyes. 'You've been having nightmares, lad. You're still feverish, I daresay. Caradoc, did you say? That's a king's name. It was in our family once. I don't know where you can have heard it, though.'

'He's the chief –' began Fred, and then changed his mind. He was too tired to try and explain any more, and in any case he didn't think anybody would believe him.

His father touched his cheek, saying, 'That's right, lad. You settle down and have a good sleep. Aunt Jen will be up with your medicine.'

There was just one more question which his father's authority in the household could answer. 'Can Alice come?' Fred asked, raising his head.

'Oh yes, I expect she'll be along after school, and Willie, too,' said his father. He waved a cheerful hand and went downstairs. Within five minutes young Fred was asleep again.

*

There was not much sleep, however, for the mice down below, though some of the little ones dropped off from time to time. They were all gathered together in the farthest corner of the cellar, in a dusty space behind a collection of empty cardboard boxes. Their light footprints had made a dancing pattern in the dust, as if there had recently been a ball. The mice sat in semi-circles, all facing Caradoc who sat in the centre with Almond at his side. Thirteen – nobody called him Singleton yet – sat in the front row with Almond's wife and her three small children who were about his own age. She was one of the chief's great-granddaughters. Thirteen's older brothers and sisters sat behind with their wives, husbands and several children. Follifoot and his four brothers were on the back row with Janus. The Cleveland-Tontines were all together, waiting for the naming of the seven little mice who had just come of age.

A soft whispering rustled up and down the ranks of mice, and an occasional high squeak from one of the children broke the sound of their murmuring. Caradoc lifted his head, raised his right paw and silence fell.

'We meet,' said Caradoc wearily but with his usual dignity, 'to discuss a plan of action. The future of our tribe is threatened, and we can no longer dwell here in safety. We

nced to find another place to live. We must, I fear, go before long. We must go together, and we must go with great caution. We must decide when and where we are going. In the meantime we must all be vigilant and take no risks. The children must be cared for, and no mouse – *no* mouse – is to go about alone or without permission. We will hear suggestions. Almond?'

'Sir,' said Almond, rising to his feet. 'We had better decide things in order. Firstly, we must travel at night, of course. The snow, if we are going outside, will give us no protection and we shall be seen very easily. And even if we travel underground from house to house, it is safer in the dark. Secondly, we must travel in groups. If we split up into parties there is a better chance of at least some of us getting safely away. Any journey is dangerous, as we all know, and we must face the risks. Thirdly, we shall need to take some kind of provisions with us. Fourthly, we must think very carefully about our destination. We can't travel too far. Some of the children will have to be carried. It is too cold to attempt to cover a great distance, so we may have to make several journeys, night after night, before we can reach a place of real safety. The thing is, where is it safe?'

A low excited chatter broke out amongst the mice.

'... cellars next door but one ... the old house in the Square ... the schoolhouse on the corner ... the chapel ... the bakehouse ...' Suggestions came from all sides, and Caradoc raised his claw once more for silence.

'The schoolhouse is unprovided with any food. Only the children who bring bread to school drop crumbs and those are swept up every afternoon by a serving woman, who washes the floor with an evil-smelling liquid. There is a dustbin outside, but the lid is always on. We could never survive there. We should starve to death.'

'The chapel's worse,' said Janus. 'My grandfather told me that he took his family there and they had nothing to eat for a week. A few broken bits of peppermint on Sundays, that's all. Blows your whiskers off, that does.'

'Next door but one,' said Arthington with a shiver, 'there's a huge ginger cat. We shouldn't last a day there, cellars or no cellars.'

'The bakehouse ... the bakehouse ... the bakehouse ...' came an insistent chorus of eager whispers.

'That's all very fine,' objected Almond, 'but there are lots of mice there already. The people are kindly enough; but if we joined that tribe it would mean depriving them of half their food, and we'd all be dreadfully crowded. Still, it's the best idea yet. Perhaps we could go there temporarily until we can find somewhere else, or until the weather breaks.'

More chattering went on among the ranks. They were all getting restless. Mice are by nature scatter-brained. Their short memories and their lack of concentration presented great difficulties to all attempts to organize any kind of plan. Caradoc and Almond were exceptional, which is why they had become accepted leaders of the tribe. The general habit of mice is to act first and think afterwards, if indeed they think at all, and these two, one of noble and ancient lineage and one of unusual intelligence, had a hard time keeping the group together.

Almond perceived that the meeting had gone as far as it could, and after consulting Caradoc he issued orders. 'We meet again tonight, here. Now all of you, keep close. Be careful. Watch your step. Look out for traps. And for goodness' sake –' but he never finished his sentence, because there was a sudden small explosion, which in this company sounded like a thunderclap.

Thirteen had sneezed. Either some dust had got into his nose, or he had been dozing off, or he had caught a cold. The noise he made was, for a mouse, surprisingly loud, and it made everybody jump. He looked abashed and embarrassed, and buried his nose in his paws.

'Bless you,' said Almond.

Caradoc looked kindly down at the little mouse, with the hint of a smile. 'A timely reminder, my friends. We must name the children before we disperse. This child, who is one of my own line, is to be named Singleton.'

Thirteen, nudged by his foster-mother and beckoned by Almond, crept up to the feet of Caradoc, who touched noses with him. With his re-naming he seemed to grow in stature. The other mice murmured, 'Singleton, Singleton,' repeating the name in a soft chorus.

There was quite a crowd of small mice lining up for the naming. One by one they approached Caradoc. Chosen names were bestowed upon them and they went proudly away, becoming, at the touch of the chief's nose and by the recognition of all the company, responsible members of the tribe. The Cleveland-Tontine children, sure enough, all received double-barrelled names. After the last little mouse had been named, Caradoc rose. Waving his paw in a gesture of dismissal, he said, 'We meet tonight; for who knows what tomorrow may bring?' There was a scurry, a whisper, a momentary sharp patter of tiny feet and then they disappeared. The mice were suddenly not there. They had retreated to the dark corners and to their own hidden places, behind the cobwebs and the dust. As far as any human eyes could see, the cellars were empty.

*

Fred's father came down the cellar steps some hours later, with one mousetrap in his hand, two more tucked under his arm, and a knob of cheese in his pocket. He set down the traps at intervals in the cellars, carefully closing the door of each one so that no mouse could be tempted in. He broke up the cheese with his fingers and scattered the crumbs about the floor.

'Good luck, little chaps,' he said as he went back up the cold stone stairs. 'Enjoy your supper. It's too cold to starve.' He swung his hurricane lantern so that its light swept the corners of the cellars, and for an instant he thought he saw a small whiskered face peering from the wainscot. He waved in its direction, and shut the cellar door behind him. The latch clicked, and all was quiet once more – as quiet as a mouse.

[5]

Alice was peeping round the door of Fred's bedroom, her face bright with cold and her dark hair tangled under her cap. She tiptoed in and sat down on the bed. Young Fred sat up and stared. He had been dozing, and was surprised to find that it was almost dark. He was also surprised that he very much wanted his tea. Alice extracted a sticky paper from her pocket and handed him a stripey mint humbug. She popped one into her own mouth and they both sat sucking contentedly and trying to talk with their mouths full.

Alice picked up the medicine bottle on Fred's table, pulled the cork out and sniffed the dark sticky mixture. 'Ugh,' she said. 'Smells like licorice.'

'It's awful,' said Fred. 'Aunt Jen puts it in hot water. Where's Willie?'

'Playing with Ben in the snow house, he was,' said Alice. 'I daresay they've gone in though. It's getting dark. Nearly tea-time.'

'Don't go yet,' said Fred anxiously. 'There's a lot to tell you. Listen –' and he told her all about Caradoc and the mice, and the trap, and his journey to the cellar, and little Thirteen, and his night visitors. The story came out in a muddle and all in the wrong order, but Alice didn't seem to mind that. Her eyes grew rounder and rounder as she listened.

'What do you mean – they talked to you? Mice can't talk. They never talk.'

'They did,' insisted Fred. 'These mice did. And they're in dreadful danger. I've been all day thinking what to do about it. Alice, you've got to help. We can't just let them die. They're not safe here and wherever can they go? Where else could they live?'

Alice twirled the last long splinter of mint humbug round on the tip of her tongue. 'In the snow house,' she said without any hesitation. 'It's just right for mice.'

'But they'd freeze to death,' protested Fred.

'Why should they?' said Alice. 'Eskimos don't. They live in snow houses.'

'Eskimos?' said Fred. 'What's Eskimos?'

'People,' said Alice cheerfully. 'They live in snow houses. They make bricks out of snow and ice and build houses and live in them. They're round,' she added helpfully. Fred was not sure whether she was referring to the people or their houses. 'We've done them at school in geography. They live in snow houses and wear fur clothes, and eat fish and seals and fight polar bears and make sledges.'

Young Fred contemplated this remarkable vision. 'But mice haven't got fur clothes to put on.'

'Yes they have, so,' said Alice firmly. 'They've grown them on. And we could give them cheese and bread instead of fish and my Dad would make them a sledge.' She jumped to her feet, her eyes shining, and clapped her hands. 'Let's do it, Fred. We could go and see them every day and they're sure to be all right. Nobody would ever know they were there, only me and you and Willie and Ben, and maybe my Dad.'

Young Fred's loyalty surged up. 'And my Dad too,' he said stoutly. 'My Dad would never hurt them.'

'Of course,' said Alice, sitting down on the end of the bed again. 'Maybe we'd better not tell any of them though. You never know what they'll say, really. But tell me again about when they came to see you.' So Fred began his recital all over again. Halfway through, Aunt Jen came up with his tea on a tray, and said she thought Alice should go home. She had, however, put an extra toasted muffin on the tray and there were two mugs of hot cocoa instead of one. So Alice stayed, and after Aunt Jen had disappeared they began to lay plans.

'Suppose they come up and see you again tonight,' said Alice, 'you can tell them about the snow house.'

'They might not, though,' said Fred in a worried voice. 'I'll have to go down to them, I daresay. Into the cellar, I mean.' He thought about this. In the cellar the mice had been – well, just mice. The fantastic encounter in his bedroom was something quite different, and Fred was not at all sure that the two worlds could ever meet. Indeed, he was not quite sure, in his heart of hearts, whether the visit of the mice had been real, or only part of his dreams. So while he chewed his toasted muffin he decided to wait and see. But he did put aside half of it, crumbled up into a buttery heap, and secreted it in the top drawer just in case. Alice added a mint humbug for luck, and they hid it all under Fred's clean shirts.

A few minutes later Fred's father came up. He took out of his overall pocket a box of wax crayons and a little book of pictures to colour. They were curious pictures and included a polar bear balanced on an iceberg, a cockatoo, a waggonette full of children carrying bunches of flowers and sheaves of corn, and a lady in a huge straw hat watering the garden. 'Pretty, aren't they?' said Alice, looking over Fred's shoulder as he turned the pages.

Dad put his hand into his other pocket, brought it out again closed in a tight fist, and pushed it under Fred's nose. 'I did that job for you,' he said, waving his fist about. 'They'll be all right tonight, your little friends, so don't you have any more nightmares. Look, I've brought you someone to keep you company.' He opened his fingers and revealed a tiny mouse, carved out of wood, balanced on a spiral spring. It jumped up and down on the table when he tapped its head.

Fred chuckled with pleasure, and his father chuckled back at him. 'Friend of Fred's,' he told Alice. 'I made it for you, lad. Don't frighten Aunt Jen with it, will you? Time you went home, young Alice. I'll walk you across the Square. It's getting late. Your Mam'll wonder where you are.'

'She knows,' said Alice, jumping up and brushing down her skirt. 'Good night, young Fred. See you tomorrow. Don't forget what we said. Uncle Fred,' she added, as she took Fred's father's hand, 'd'you believe mice can talk?'

'Young Fred does,' he said, smiling down at her bright face, 'so I know he must have been talking whether mice can or not. I think he's having dreams and nightmares.'

'I don't,' said Alice decidedly. 'I think they talk, I do. They must talk. People talk. You talk. I talk. Willie talks all the time. Why shouldn't mice talk? And cats and dogs and all, for that matter? Let's go. I'll ask my Dad. Good night Fred.' And Alice, eagerly chattering, hand in hand with Fred's father, went jigging down the stairs. They met Aunt Jen halfway.

'I'll be up again soon,' Fred's father sang out cheerfully; and Fred heard Aunt Jen's retreating footsteps and her anxious muttering.

'Bad luck to pass on the stairs. That boy needs his sleep. He gets too excited ... just like his mother, he is ...' His father's and Alice's footsteps receded and Aunt Jen's came back again, into his bedroom.

' 'Night, Alice,' he called in a croaking voice that broke up into a cough.

'There you are, you see,' said Aunt Jen. 'What did I tell you? Too excited by half, and that cough on your chest. You'll have a bad night, I shouldn't wonder. I'd better come up and see you're all right later on.'

Young Fred, horror-stricken at the prospect of being visited by Aunt Jen during the night, choked and coughed and spluttered. He looked at her under eyelids deliberately drooping. 'I'm awful sleepy, Aunt Jen,' he croaked piteously. 'Can I have a hot brick? And a drink, please?'

Aunt Jen looked at him suspiciously. 'I've brought you both, my lad, and well you know it. Here.' She pushed the hot brick into the bottom of his bed. 'I've brought you a lemon drink,' she said reproachfully, and proceeded to feed it to him in small sips. Fred relaxed into his pillow, battling against sleep. 'Oh please,' he thought, 'please don't let her come when the mice are here. Please let me wake up

36

when they come and let me be by myself.' The little wooden mouse his father had carved for him was tucked under his pillow, and his hand curled protectively round it.

'Will you leave the light for a bit, Aunt Jen please?' he pleaded. 'Dad's coming back – he said.' So, though she did not really approve, Aunt Jen allowed him to keep his candle burning, and after she had gone downstairs Fred lay and watched the spire of flame, and made the little wooden mouse dance in the circle of light, while he spoke to it lovingly. 'Singleton,' he said. 'Little Singleton. You're a singleton too, like me and Thirteen. That's three of us.' He was leaning up on his elbow, tapping the jumping mouse with his finger, and he did not see his father standing in the doorway behind his bed. Dad had crept upstairs in his stockinged feet in case Fred was asleep, and stood quietly watching him.

'The little lad's lonely,' he thought to himself. 'He misses his Mam.' Pushing his hat back on his head and scratching his ear, he spoke softly, not wanting to startle the boy. 'Talking to yourself, young Fred? Or talking to your mouse? How about talking to your Dad for a change?'

He sat down by the pillow, and his arm went round Fred's shoulders. He picked up the little wooden mouse and looked at it critically. 'I could have made a better job of it,' he said, 'but I didn't have much time today. What with doing your errands for you –' he poked his fingers into Fred's ribs, 'and the shop was busy. Still, he'll do. What did you call him? Singleton, was it? If you knew as much as I do about mice, my lad, you'd not call him Singleton. They run to large families, mice do. Only I didn't have time to make a family of them for you, did I, eh?'

'Oh, Dad, he's lovely. And I don't want a family. Sometimes they do have a singleton. Like Thirteen – he's one on his own.'

Fred's father pushed his hat even further back on his

37

head. 'Talk sense,' he said. 'How can you have a singleton if there are thirteen? Whatever do they teach you at school?'

Fred could not attempt an explanation. He opened his mouth to try, but gave it up as impossible. Then he said with a sudden inspiration, 'What's a baker's dozen, Dad?'

His father threw back his head with a huge laugh like Uncle John's, and hugged the boy's shoulder. He said, 'That's a good answer. One extra. You're a clever lad, and no mistake. But mice – I doubt it. It's not in nature really. And now, young Fred, if you don't go off to sleep and I don't go downstairs, your Aunt Jen will be after both of us. So, no more of these fairy stories. You lie down. Here's your Singleton to keep you company,' he put the little wooden mouse by the pillow. 'Go to sleep now, young Fred. You'll be fine in the morning, I daresay, ready to colour your drawing book so that I can take it to show Mam, eh?'

'Oh Dad,' said Fred with sudden longing, 'I wish I could come with you.'

'So do I, lad. And so does Mam. It'll be a poor do without you. But they won't let children in, you know that. It's the first time they've let me in, so when I go on Saturday I expect they won't let me stay long.' He blew softly into Fred's ear, got up rather wearily, and stood for a moment by the candle, twinkling at his small son. 'Pouff ... and out it goes.' He pinched the black smoking wick between his finger and thumb, wiped his fingers down his long-suffering overall, and moved, soft-footed in his stockings, towards the bedroom door. A thin spiral of smoke from the dead candle curvetted towards the ceiling, and the smell of hot wax assailed Fred's nose.

'Good night, young Fred,' his father's voice came from the doorway. And then very softly, 'Good night, my bonny lad.' The door was left open and the light of the oil lamp on the stairs gleamed into the bedroom. Dad went quietly downstairs, and Fred was left alone to sort out his secret problems.

Somehow or other, the mice had to be rescued. It was a major exercise in planning and Fred needed to apply all his powers to it. So he did not go to sleep. He was able, however, to pretend. When he heard Aunt Jen creeping in to look at him he kept his eyes tight shut until she had crept away, wholly satisfied that he was sound asleep. But his mind was working it all out, and after she had gone he sat bolt upright in bed, thinking hard.

In the bakehouse across the Square, Alice lay awake. She was thinking too.

[6]

'And so,' said Caradoc to Fred, 'the matter is urgent. We have twenty-four hours.'

The mice had arrived just before dawn. They were less talkative than on the previous night, and seemed dispirited and somewhat bewildered, except for little Singleton who took up his position confidently beside Fred's thumb. Caradoc and Almond between them had explained the situation to Fred. Three traps, said Caradoc, had appeared in the cellars that day. Mercifully they were already sprung and there was no lure of cheese in them, though neither he nor Almond could understand why. There had been cheese crumbs scattered about on the floor, which was equally puzzling, but seemed on the whole both harmless and helpful.

'Good old Dad,' thought Fred, hugging himself, though Arthington was muttering darkly about the possibility of poison.

But the very presence of the traps was enough. By universal consent the mice had decided that it was time for them to move on, and they would not listen to Fred's explanation. The only thing they had not decided was where – or 'whither', as Caradoc put it in his old-fashioned diction – to go. These facts were put before Fred, clearly and briefly. The company of mice then fell silent and awaited his reply. Their pointed faces all turned to Fred in hope and faith. It was a terrifying responsibility he had to carry. He took a long deep breath and began to speak.

'You can have our snow house to live in if you want it. Alice and me, we think it's just right for you. It's in the Square outside between the bakehouse and The Sundial. Uncle John made it out of our snowball. There are windows and doors so you can go in and out and there's room for all of you inside. Nobody else can get in. It's too small for people but it's a big place really. Alice and Willie and Ben and me, we can bring you your supper every night and nobody else will know you're there. It's a lovely house, like a palace all made of ice. Eskimos,' he added, boasting of his new knowledge, 'Eskimos live in snow houses. You'd be all right. It's ours. We'd look after you. And there'd be no traps.'

There was a long silence after Fred's breathless speech. The mice had all listened attentively, and they now turned to Caradoc and Almond who were talking together in undertones. At last Caradoc spoke.

'We are more grateful than we can tell you,' he said gravely, 'and we shall, as a tribe, be forever in your debt. We are accustomed to fending for ourselves and would not wish to impose upon your charity. In our straitened circumstances, however –'

Almond saw Fred's puzzled expression and hastily interrupted. 'Excuse me, Sir,' he said. 'Put it this way. We shall be very glad of your help and this snow house of yours sounds a jolly good idea, at least for the time being. We could move out tomorrow night. Arthington and I will organize it. If you could collect a few provisions to see us through the first day, we'll be able to manage for ourselves after that, somehow.'

'Oh yes,' gasped Fred eagerly. 'I can get cheese and cake and oatmeal and biscuits and –'

'That's plenty,' said Almond firmly, glaring at the younger mice who were trembling with greedy excitement. 'Now this is what we need to do. You lay a trail of crumbs from the cellar window to the snow house, so that we know where to go. After dark, mind. The birds will eat the lot if you don't wait till after dark, and then where shall we be? We'll set out in marching order about midnight, in groups, as I said before. Scouts will be posted along the route to keep an eye on things, especially on the children to make sure they don't eat the crumbs on the way. Caradoc and I, with a small party, will bring up the rear. We shall see everybody safely away, collect up the crumbs, rub out our footprints and make sure that we are not followed. If you look in the day after tomorrow, with any luck you'll find us in the snow house.'

It sounded a splendid plan, and Fred was delighted to see that the mice were already more cheerful. Little Singleton was dancing up and down in his excitement, just like Fred's wooden mouse on its bouncing spring.

Suddenly, just as everything seemed to be turning out well, there was a soft padding of feet outside the open door. Through the doorway, from the shadows, there appeared a black furry face with two luminous eyes, long whiskers, and a small white tuft under the chin. Stepping softly with tail erect, fur shining and pink nose twitching, came Puss.

Fred's heart turned a somersault in his stomach and dropped with a sickening thump right down to his feet. Frozen with horror and unable to think or speak, he shut his eyes and covered them with his hands. He waited, for what seemed an eternity, for the shrieks of mice being murdered, and for the scampering feet of his panic-stricken friends, who, because of his own lack of forethought, had all been endangered. He waited, with a terrible helpless dread, for the end of the world.

'Good evening, Puss,' said Caradoc in his most courteous tone. 'It is some time since we had the pleasure of your company. How is the family?'

Fred opened his eyes in astonishment and disbelief. There on the coverlet before him lay Puss, purring happily, stretching and flexing her paws, while a score of little brown mice scrambled over her with squeaks of delight. Only the baby mice cowered away; some clustering behind Almond and others crouching round Arthington. Singleton had fled away from Fred's hand and was close to Caradoc, his whiskers trembling. And wonder of wonders, Puss began to speak.

'The kittens are well, thank you,' she said. 'Growing fast, of course. I've left them upstairs.' Puss, as Fred well knew, always kept her kittens in the loft. 'But whatever are you doing here with our Fred?' She rubbed her head lovingly against Fred's knees. He was still speechless with surprise, but Caradoc and Almond recounted to Puss the story of the traps and the plans for departure, and Singleton's rescue.

'This is my young relative,' said Caradoc, pushing the shivering little mouse forward towards Puss. 'The boy saved his life. Now go along, child. You are quite safe.'

Puss sniffed at Singleton's ears and licked his nose with the tip of her pink tongue, and the little mouse's eyes almost popped out of his head. The other infant mice were sent up to Puss and received the same gentle greeting.

'Your numbers seem to be growing fast,' said Puss to Caradoc. 'It is as well I called in. But I must say I feel a little upset that you should think of moving away without telling me. I might be able to give you a hand, you know.'

Caradoc was quick to apologize and explain. 'We did not wish to intrude on your privacy when you had newborn children to care for,' he said. 'We should, of course, have sent a message later on.'

By this time Fred had found his voice. 'Puss!' he cried.

'Puss! I never knew you could talk. I never knew you liked mice. Why ... why don't you eat them?'

Puss looked offended, and Caradoc hastily explained. 'We did Puss a small service in the past,' he said in some embarrassment, 'and we have enjoyed her friendship ever since.'

'Caradoc's father and some of the family saved the life of one of my kittens,' said Puss. 'She was caught in a noose of string in the cellar and would have choked to death if they hadn't all gnawed through the string and set her free. It was her own fault, of course, silly creature. She's grown up now and gone away. I expect she's just as silly. She never would listen to what she was told. But that was a long time ago. As for talking – why shouldn't I talk? If you could learn to purr and miaow and squeak you'd know a lot more than you do at present, young Fred. Well, I'd better be getting back to my kittens. I only came in because I heard all this chattering and wondered what was going on. If you take my advice you'll go too, Caradoc. Aunt Jen's not sleeping at all soundly. I heard her tossing about and muttering. I'll keep an eye open for you when you go on your journey. Good luck. Watch out for that pug across the street. He's often loose at night and I wouldn't trust him as far as I can see him. He has an ugly upside-down sort of nose. Good night, all.' Puss paused to stretch up and rub her face against Fred's cheek before she leapt gracefully to the ground. 'Don't worry, young Fred,' she murmured in a vibrant purring voice. 'We've all been here a long time. You've got a bit of fever, you know.'

'I'm not dreaming,' cried Fred desperately, very much afraid that he was, and would wake up any moment. 'I'm not.' But Puss had vanished into the darkness with a flick of her tail. The mice began to scuttle and slither to the floor, and very soon all except Caradoc, Almond, Arthington and Singleton had departed.

'I'll tell you something, Almond,' said Arthington. 'We'll need to watch those young bloods from the Otley family. Think they're too clever by half, all of them. Did you notice them when you were giving out the orders? Sitting in the corner sniggering and giggling and paying no attention at all. We shall have trouble with them before we've finished, I'll be bound.'

'I'll have a word with them down below,' said Almond. He was anxious to be gone, but Caradoc hesitated, and then turned to Fred. 'We will meet again in your snow house, all being well,' he said. 'For the present, farewell. Who knows what tomorrow may bring?' His voice was very quiet, and the ticking of the clock downstairs almost drowned his words. He raised a paw in greeting, and was gone, like a minute shadow. Almond and Arthington followed him closely. Fred's eyes were stinging as he wondered if he would ever really see any of them again. Little Singleton came racing back to him, and looking up, plucked at his finger with a tiny sharp claw. A tear rolled down Fred's cheek and fell like a raindrop on the top of Singleton's head, startling him.

'Goodbye,' whispered Fred. 'Good luck.' And the little mouse, who had never yet spoken, squeaked, jumped high into the air, and disappeared.

[7]

Young Fred did not, of course, see any of the events of the journey from The Sundial to the snow house the following night. His bedroom window looked out on to the street and not on to the Square. He was still what Aunt Jen called 'bedfast'. He had not been allowed up during the day, and did not dare risk either creeping out of the house at night or even visiting the cellars in case he woke anybody and wrecked the whole undertaking.

The day had seemed as though it would never end, in spite of his many visitors. The doctor had called just before midday, pronounced Fred much improved, and suggested that he should be allowed up for his dinner the next day. 'What good's that?' thought Fred miserably. 'It's today that matters.' But Dr James waved away his pleadings with his twirling spectacles and told his father that he was too thin and pale by half. Dad had been up to talk to him half a dozen times, bringing a succession of gifts – a small sweet orange, a handful of jelly babies, and a stick of coltsfoot rock which he stuck into Fred's mouth, complaining ruefully that he might get more conversation out of the little wooden mouse than he got out of his preoccupied son. He sat on the bed, and taking a piece of paper out of his overall pocket he folded and twisted it with deft speed into a tiny paper boat. Then with a grin at Fred, he suddenly turned it inside out and changed it into a diminutive cocked hat which he set at a rakish angle on the toy mouse's head. In spite of his anxiety, Fred laughed.

'That's better,' said Dad, making the mouse dance on its wire. He pushed his own hat back on his head. 'Don't fret, lad. You'll be up and about and playing out in your snow house in a day or two.'

Aunt Jen, of course, had been up and down incessantly. She produced food and drink and washing and medicine, advice and worry. She came often but never stayed long, and was more of an interruption than a visitor. Alice came at last, after school, and Fred recounted all the previous night's events and described the astonishing encounter with Puss. Alice listened wide-eyed, and promised to see that there would be bread for the crumb-trail and a little store of food in the snow house when night came. Then Uncle John came in to see how Fred was and to fetch Alice home. He brought a little round cake shaped like a snowball, coated with sugar and coconut, for Fred's tea. It was still warm and smelt delicious.

'Just out of the oven,' said Uncle John, 'so it's not as cold as it looks. Come on, young Alice. Yours is on the table waiting for you.'

And after that, the day was nearly over. Apart from Aunt Jen, and his father, who looked in to say good night, Fred had only one more visitor. Puss herself strolled in while he was having his supper. She leapt on to the bed and lay across Fred's knees, purring softly. Fred caressed her shining head and whispered in her twitching ear.

'Oh Puss, Puss,' he murmured, 'Did you really talk? Why don't you talk now? Talk to me, Puss, talk to me.'

Puss gazed at him with half-shut golden eyes, and continued to purr. He dipped his finger into his drink of warm sweet milk, and she delicately licked it dry. Then she got up, stretched, and went off back to her kittens, saying never a word.

'That cat,' said Aunt Jen as she came bustling in for the last time. 'It's dangerous, creeping about in the dark. Nearly had me over just now. And what good does it do, I'd like to know? Too well fed. Never goes after the mice. Might as well not keep a cat.' She muttered on, and Fred was thankful when she tucked him in, blew the candle out, and left him in the dark. And he had to stay in bed, wide awake and wondering, and trust to Alice to carry out Almond's instructions that he had carefully reported to her. So he did not hear the full story until later, and even then he had to piece it together from various accounts.

*

The grandfather clock in the kitchen struck twelve – a rather rusty, husky twelve, and as the distant echo of the last stroke died away in the cellars, Almond and Arthington

47

assembled all the mice in orderly groups, while Caradoc sat on a shelf, a remote but respected commander-in-chief.

'Now,' said Almond, running a careful eye over the ranks, 'we'll go through the plans and all the instructions. Scouts and group-leaders, forward.'

Follifoot, and Arthington's other three brothers, and the older Cleveland-Tontines, scampered to the front, and stood before Almond awaiting orders. As Almond had said to Caradoc when they were planning the expedition, the Cleveland-Tontines might have big ideas about their social status but you could always rely on them in an emergency.

'Is the trail laid?' asked Arthington anxiously. 'Have you put out the crumbs so that everyone can follow the right road?'

'We laid it two hours ago,' answered Follifoot. 'Puss had already let us know that young Fred could not do it for us. The girl Alice tried to help us, but she was interrupted. She did however leave several slices of bread at the top of the cellar steps outside the window, so we broke it up ourselves, and ten of us scattered the crumbs to make a trail from The Sundial to the snow house. It took a long time. It was brown bread – very thoughtful, Alice is – and it shows up better against the snow. It had currants in it,' he added wistfully, 'and it smelt delicious. The ones who bring up the rear will have the benefit of it because they will have to eat up the crumbs on the way.'

'Nobody else, mind,' said Almond severely. 'Not a mouse must touch a crumb except the children who will travel together at the end, and their guardians. They will all keep close together and eat up the crumbs as they come, removing all traces of our journey. I doubt,' he said in an undertone to Arthington, 'whether anybody could stop the children eating, so they'll have to come last.' He raised his voice again. 'Five guards will ensure that our footprints are all rubbed out. Who are they?'

Five mice stepped forward and saluted. 'The Dewsbury family,' said Almond. 'That's good. But we need not worry, I think, about food. Alice promised that a supply would be put in the snow house for us, and she is a reliable girl.'

'Cake, perhaps,' began Janus hopefully, and then looked ashamed as all the mice lifted their noses. 'Sorry,' he muttered hastily to Almond.

Caradoc spoke gently and kindly from the shelf where he was crouching. 'Everyone is hungry. It is understandable that the thought of food may distract us. We need to be very wary, disciplined and restrained. Whatever we have, we must all share.'

Almond went on with his orders. 'Follifoot and Tontine know the way, so they will lead us. The head of each family is responsible for his group, and the families will proceed along the trail, keeping in sight of each other, quietly, as fast as possible but in a perfectly orderly manner. The children, in charge of their mothers or some other responsible person, wait until last. Arthington and I will go last of all.'

All this time Arthington had been scanning the lines of mice, and was looking more and more anxious. 'We're not all here,' he muttered. 'There's somebody missing.' He stared along the lines again, checking up on the children particularly. Then, 'I knew it. I knew we'd have trouble. It's the Otley lot. They haven't turned up. All seven of them. Where can they be?'

Almond hastily ran his eye along the ranks, and saw that Arthington was right. He turned to Caradoc. 'Sir, there are seven of us missing – the young Otleys. The children are here but Calverley and his brothers and their four cousins are absent.'

Caradoc was perturbed. 'Surely,' he said, 'no disaster can have befallen them. We have kept close all day and hardly left our holes. What can have happened?'

Arthington snorted. 'Mark my words, they're either

asleep or they've gone off somewhere without permission. Now I suppose we shall have to send out a search party.'

The mice stirred uneasily. They were already nervous enough, and this new problem produced great agitation. Almond himself was both worried and angry.

'I'll go myself,' he said, 'and I'd like the Dewsburys to come with me. We'll search the holes and corners and call as loudly as we dare. Come on. We haven't much time.'

The six mice scampered away. They scuttled hither and thither, their high squeaks urgently summoning the missing mice; but there was no response: the young Otleys were nowhere to be found. Almond and his companions returned at last with cobwebs and dust on their whiskers to report their failure.

'Not a sight nor sound of them,' said Almond. 'They seem to have disappeared. We've looked everywhere.'

Caradoc rose sadly to his feet. 'We can delay no longer,' he said. 'I fear our young friends will have to fend for themselves. We must be on our way. I, of course, shall be the last to leave and I will keep a constant look-out for them. I fancy we may also have a friend to help us.'

'Oh yes, Caradoc, Sir,' said Follifoot eagerly. 'Puss was with us when we put out the crumbs, and she promised to be in the Square at midnight.'

'Midnight is already long past,' said Caradoc urgently. 'We must make haste. Our journey must begin at once. Good fortune go with us all – away, away.'

The mice stood up and began to form themselves into their travelling groups. The semi-circles dissolved into long lines, with Follifoot and the oldest Cleveland-Tontines at the head. The children were all assembled at the back with their mothers. Some of the smallest mice were beginning to whimper, and their mothers scolded and comforted them by turns. The tiniest babies were picked up by friends and relations and carried. Each group of children had an older mouse for a guard. Janus, at Almond's request, stationed himself apart from the rest, ready to run up and down the ranks and keep a look-out for any danger. They were all ready, and just about to set out, when there was a sudden disturbance in the remote shadows. The mice all swung round in that direction, drawing back in fear at what they saw.

Down the cellar steps came Puss, eyes ablaze and whiskers trembling. A kicking, struggling mouse hung from her mouth, and six other mice were running wildly before her, shrieking with terror.

The whole company was transfixed with horror. Puss looked enormous, her golden eyes gleaming and her padding feet coming rapidly towards them, the image of the ancient enemy of mice. Caradoc himself stared at her in disbelief, a terrible dread shaking his heart. For a moment he could not move, but then his courage rose. He ran to the head of the column and stood his ground, facing the oncoming cat. Puss, preceded by the six scampering mice, came straight up to him and dropped the struggling mouse at his feet. The little creature rolled over, lay still for a second, then made an attempt to stand. It reeled, and sat down on its haunches with a foolish expression on its face. The others slid to a halt in front of Caradoc, and crouched before him in a heap. Puss looked down at them distastefully, sat down herself, and began to clean her whiskers.

'Oh, my goodness,' said Arthington. 'It's young Calverley and he's been at the whisky again.'

Puss paused in her ablutions and looked at Caradoc. 'I found them in the shop,' she said. 'They'd eaten through a cork and were lapping up the spirit. He,' looking at the mouse who was sitting on the floor, rocking backwards and forwards, 'was singing.'

If any mouse could have produced a voice like thunder Caradoc would have done so then. He glowered between drawn brows at the drunken culprits, his eyes dark with anger, and addressed them coldly with ancient authority.

'Your behaviour is graceless and your conduct deplorable. You have put us all in grave danger. Your own lives could well have been lost had it not been for Puss's great friendship. This friendship you certainly do not deserve. You are a disgrace not only to our own tribe but to the whole race of mice. I am tempted to leave you to a fate you wholly deserve, but, for the sake of your forefathers, I will offer you one more chance of our protection. You will travel with us, but under guard. You, young man,' glaring at Calverley, 'are obviously incapable of walking so you will have to be carried with the children. We need volunteers for this unpleasant task.' Calverley giggled weakly, and two grim-faced mice stepped forward to take him away. A group of others escorted the rest of the young Otleys to the back of the column.

Caradoc looked sadly at Puss, shaking his tired old head. 'You could destroy us all,' he said, 'and for a dreadful moment, in my fear, I must confess I thought it was in your mind. It was a most unworthy thought. Forgive me, my old friend. What should we do without you? How can we ever thank you?'

Puss touched his nose with hers, very gently. 'By getting on with the job,' she said. 'I had to frighten them, and it meant frightening everybody else, too. Think nothing of it. But you must go, if you're going. It's very late.'

The broken ranks reformed themselves, and Almond issued his final orders. The mice scurried up the cellar steps, round the door which had been left ajar, and, creeping with hardly a sound through the dark shop, squeezed themselves under the door and out into the cold snowy night. Young Fred, straining his ears upstairs, heard not a patter nor a squeak.

*

Alice had been watching and waiting at the window of her bedroom since eleven o'clock. Little Ben had been put to bed at seven and Willie at eight, and she had managed to keep her parents talking for a full hour past her own bed-time, until at last her mother hustled her upstairs with a mug of hot cocoa and a ginger biscuit and a candle.

'Go to sleep now, child, like a good girl. Your tongue is as long as a tailor's tape.'

Left alone in the candlelight, Alice sipped her cocoa and nibbled her biscuit as slowly as she could, and kept her candle burning as long as she dared, afraid of falling asleep and missing all the excitement. So far she had told nobody about the mice, and though she had been sorely tempted to let Willie into the secret, she had thought better of it because she was afraid his bubbling chatter might give the game away. When she heard her parents stirring downstairs and getting ready to come to bed, she hastily blew out the candle, pinched the smoking wick, and snuggled down under the covers. Ten minutes later, when her mother looked in, she was apparently fast asleep, breathing deeply. Ten minutes after that she was sitting up again, listening intently. She heard the movements and the murmur of voices die away, and soon she heard her father snoring. Safe at last, she crept out of bed, wrapped herself in her patchwork dressing-gown, put a blanket round her shoulders and settled down at the window to wait. The Square was dark, except for the glimmer of the moon and a host of frosty stars. It was very cold. She tucked the blanket close to stop herself shivering. She began to get sleepy, and her consciousness seemed to ebb and flow in her efforts to keep awake.

She must have gone to sleep after all, she told Fred the next day, because her body was quite stiff when she stretched her eyes open and became aware that something was going on outside. She leaned forward, her nose against the window, and peered out into the night. She could see the huge globe of the snow house shining like a palace with its dark windows and door and the shadowy carriage drive. And in the far distance, from the back door of The Sundial, she saw what looked like a ball of dark string unwinding itself across the Square. As she stared, she could make out the running, jumping, scampering movements of tiny creatures. The unwinding ball of string came nearer, and now Alice could see two files of mice scuttering across the snow, their noses to the ground, following the trail of crumbs that had been laid earlier on. Mice never run straight, and the trail had been laid in a sinuous curve. The moving string followed it, and Alice held her breath as she watched. It was

a long way for such small creatures to go, and every inch of
the way carried danger. The long procession wove its way
onwards, and it was led, suddenly, not by the courageous
Follifoot and his companions (though Alice did not know
their names) but by a huge dancing curvetting shape. Alice
was spellbound. The one thing she had not really believed
in was the friendship of Puss. She stared in amazement at
the graceful cat who had emerged from a neighbouring
doorway and was guiding the mice to safety. Puss sometimes
pranced ahead and sometimes turned back to run alongside.
In any case she was a dark protective angel preserving the
feet of the travellers who could have been her natural prey.
Tears ran down Alice's cold cheeks as she watched; tears of
relief, anxiety, affection and astonishment. She rubbed the
back of her hand across her eyes so that she could see better.

The mice at the head of the column had got more than
halfway across the Square by the time the little ones, accompanied by their mothers and a few guards, emerged from
The Sundial. The children of course travelled more slowly,
and though, as Alice could see, the guards were urging them
on, the end of the line was becoming ragged and broken.
There were also some other bigger mice at the rear, who, although Alice could not know it, were the dissolute Otleys
and young Calverley, who was still hopelessly drunk. They
were straggling about in all directions in spite of the efforts
of their escorts to keep them together. Three small figures
remained by The Sundial – Caradoc, Arthington and
Almond. They were going to make a run for it when everybody else was safe.

Then all at once, a wild barking splintered the silence of
the night, and a cannon-ball hurtled itself into the line of
scampering mice. Bouncer, the pug with the 'ugly upside-
down nose' described by Puss, had materialized from nowhere and was attacking the whole company. The column
broke. Mice scattered in all directions, fleeing in terror from

the red-eyed aggressor. For a few moments there was chaos and confusion as Bouncer leaped about, jumping and snarling at the scuttling mice, his head jerking and turning, his eyes glowing, his dreadful teeth bared. Then, just as suddenly, a black furry shape flung itself into his path. Puss was there, all claws and teeth and lashing tail and upstanding fur. Bouncer's attention was distracted, and battle between the black cat and the brindled dog was joined. Bouncer was growling in his throat and Puss was spitting and snarling. They circled each other, bitter enemies, ready to fight to the death.

'Oh mercy !' Alice gave a little scream, clapped her hands over her ears, and throwing caution to the winds she raced downstairs, dragged back the bolt on the bakehouse door and dashed out into the Square, her bright patchwork dressing-gown flying behind her. The cold air made her gasp, but she ran on towards the battlefield where Puss and Bouncer were engaged in mortal combat. Little dark shapes of scurrying mice were darting in all directions, their ranks completely broken and disordered. Follifoot and his brothers had turned back in a brave but hopeless effort to gather the company together. Three of the Cleveland-Tontines, squeaking instructions, scampered into the outfield and tried to direct the panic-stricken mice back towards the snow house. But it was no use. They all ran hither and thither, forgetting everything, overcome by their desperate fear.

Alice reached the arena where Puss and the pug were fighting furiously. Puss had a torn ear and a bleeding leg. Bouncer's right eye was swollen and closed like a prizefighter's, with the marks of claws across it. The long deep tracks of Puss's claws were also visible across his rump, which was dripping blood. Just as Alice arrived, Puss drew back, snarling and spitting. She was already badly wounded and would in the end have been no match for the pug, whose solid weight threatened to bear her to the ground every time he charged. She moved like a dancer, but he fell upon her like a rock.

Puss was at the end of her tether, gasping for breath, but grimly holding on. Bouncer gathered himself, ready to spring. Alice pulled off her red slipper and hurled it at the crouching dog. It caught him on the nose, and he jumped sideways in surprise. At the same instant he caught sight of the huddle of baby mice crouching together close to The Sundial's door. He abandoned the fight with Puss, and bounded towards the children, galloping with the speed of a tornado to attack a much easier prey, his hot tongue lolling out, his bulging eyes red with rage. The little group of defenceless mice shrank closer together, shut their eyes tight, and almost stopped breathing. Alice was rooted to the spot, frozen with a new terror.

In a flash of fur and whiskers Puss was in pursuit. She seemed to fly across the Square, her paws scarcely touching the ground. Just as Bouncer reached the group of baby mice she was on his back, clawing, biting, scratching. The dog tried to shake her off but she hung on grimly. He turned and twisted, and for a moment Puss lost her grip and Bouncer turned on her, his weight bearing her down and his cruel teeth tearing at her fur. Then, without warning, there was a new diversion. Almond leapt from the doorway on to Bouncer's tail and, gripping it with all his four paws, he began to bite it savagely, as fierce and as fearless as any rat. Bouncer, attacked so unexpectedly from behind, grunted and shook himself. Puss struggled to her feet again and returned to the fray, exhausted as she was. As he felt the teeth of both cat and mouse sinking into him, Bouncer began to whine and scream. He struggled and fought, but was no match for the two ferocious assailants who were fighting for more than their lives. With a last desperate effort the pug managed to shake them off, and slunk away, wounded and bleeding, to the safety of his own house.

Puss dropped, panting to the ground, shook her head, and began to wash herself. Almond, however, lay on the snow unable to move. Alice came to him, and lifted him tenderly in her hands. He gave a little groan. Bouncer's teeth had bitten through his leg, which hung limp and helpless, the delicate bone crushed and broken.

Alice bent her face close to Almond's. His eyes were closed, and he lay unconscious. 'Dead,' thought Alice, while tears of pity and admiration ran down her cheeks.

A small voice squeaked in her ear as she knelt in the snow, cradling Almond in her hands. Caradoc was beside her, speaking urgently. 'Take him, please, to your snow house. We will gather there as soon as we can, and we will do what is right for him.'

Moving at a remarkable speed for one so old, Caradoc left her, reached the middle of the Square, and stood with his forepaw uplifted in a strange sort of command. Slowly, the mice came creeping towards him and waited for him to speak. Not until they had all assembled, and the baby mice had been brought to join the company, did he move. Then he turned and, walking slowly, led the ragged column of obedient mice over the snow to safety. Gathering up the scattered crumbs on their way, they trotted after him through the snow gate, up the little carriage drive and, one by one, disappeared into the snow house.

Alice watched them go, holding the lifeless body of Almond in her hands. Then she followed the mice to the snow house, with one foot bare because she had lost her slipper, hardly noticing how cold it was.

'And what do you think, young Fred?' she said the next morning when she told him the whole story. 'My Dad came to the door and saw me. He looked real fierce standing there, and I thought he was going to shout at me. He came striding after me and picked me up and carried me home. It was lovely and warm indoors and it was bitter cold outside. I still had the mouse, you see. I thought he was dead. My Dad took him from me and put him on the rug by the fire. "What've you got there, my lass?" he said to me, and I cried, because I thought the mouse was dead. But my Dad, he picked him up and had a look at him, and do you know what he did? He made two little splints out of his pipe spills and bound up the mouse's leg.'

Fred was desperate with anxiety. 'You keep on saying "the mouse, the mouse",' he said. 'Which mouse? What did he look like?'

Alice considered a moment. 'Well, he was brown, and he had black hairs under his chin, and an extra long tail, I think.'

'That was Almond,' cried Fred in anguish. 'So go on, Alice. What happened next?'

'Well, then my Dad got a little glass tube with a rubber bulb on the end and he warmed some milk for me and he dropped a little drop into the mouse's mouth and, would you believe it, the mouse opened his eyes and swallowed some milk. He nearly choked, though. He looked at me, Almond did, but he didn't say anything. Dad left him by the fire and took me back to bed and I went off to sleep, I was so tired. This morning I missed school. I didn't wake up in time. When I came down I looked for the mouse but he wasn't there. I asked my Dad where the mouse was and he just said "What mouse? Don't you go looking for mice in the middle of the night." So I don't know, Fred, where he can be. Mam said I'd been dreaming, but I know I hadn't, because I only had one of my slippers this morning. I couldn't find the other in the Square, though, the one I threw at Bouncer. Somebody must have taken it.'

'But what about all the mice?' asked Fred. 'Aren't they in the snow house?'

Alice was very distressed. 'I couldn't see,' she said. 'I had a look through the windows but it's so dark inside. I called to them but I couldn't hear anything. Nobody answered.'

'They don't seem to talk in the daytime,' said Fred thoughtfully. 'We'll have to wait till it's night. Aunt Jen says I can get up for dinner. She won't let me out, though. I wonder if I can get out tonight when everybody's asleep.'

'If the mice are there,' said Alice, 'we'll have to take them something. They'll be starving.'

'I saved my bread from breakfast,' Fred said. 'It's in the drawer. And I might get something from the cellar. There's some little apples in the barrel and some oatmeal in the bin. Oh hush – here's Aunt Jen coming.'

Aunt Jen bustled in with a jug of hot water. 'Now Alice, it's time you went home for your dinner. Fred's going to have a good wash and come downstairs. You'll want a clean shirt.' She poured the water into the bowl and stumped over to the chest of drawers, pulled open a drawer, and shook out a grey flannel shirt. And then – 'What in mercy's name is this, boy?'

Dropping the shirt on the bed, she took out from the drawer two slices of bread and butter folded together in a sandwich, and held them up between a distasteful finger and thumb. Young Fred's face grew scarlet as he met Aunt Jen's accusing eye. 'I – I couldn't eat it all,' he stammered. 'I saved it for later.'

'Saved it?' said Aunt Jen. 'Saved it? Anybody would think I was going to starve you all day. Bread in a drawer, indeed! No wonder there's mice all over the place – and butter on your shirt, I shouldn't wonder.' She shook the shirt out again, peering at it suspiciously. 'Well, it seems all right. Now I shall have to do the drawers out, as if there weren't enough to do. Bread in a drawer – whatever next. Now you get washed and dressed and come down to your dinner. And Alice, off you go home.'

Hustling Alice ahead of her, she went out, holding the offending sandwich at arm's length, sniffing disapprovingly.

Fred got out of bed and slowly began to wash his face. As he rubbed it dry, he turned and saw Puss coming in. 'Oh, dear,' he said. 'Oh, Puss, don't you know where the mice are?' He stooped to rub her chin, and as she winced, he saw that there were deep marks of teeth on her leg and a large tuft of fur missing from her shoulder. 'You do know, Puss, don't you?' he whispered as he very carefully caressed her head. 'Tell me, Puss, please tell me.'

But Puss only looked at him, stretched, climbed stiffly on to the bed, closed her eyes, and began to purr.

[8]

Fred did not see Alice again that day. He waited all afternoon, hoping she would come in, and could not settle down to anything.

'For goodness' sake, boy,' said Aunt Jen in exasperation, 'can't you sit down and look at your books or something? You keep wandering about under my feet like a lost soul. Worse than young Willie, you are.'

At last Fred went into the shop and pottered about behind the counter. His father was particularly busy weighing out a consignment of sugar into bags between serving customers with the weekend orders. He glanced at Fred's pale and troubled face, and put a pile of stiff blue sugar bags in front of him.

'Here, lad. Open these out for me, will you? Then you can put the sugar in. There's the scoop. Pound in each, and mind you weigh it properly. I'll be in trouble if anybody finds it short.'

Fred spread out the bags and began to fill them with the soft brown sugar from the sack. It flowed solidly into the bags in a thick heavy stream, and Fred's sticky fingers tasted sweet when he licked them. Some of the sugar spilt on to the floor and crunched under his feet. 'If only the mice were here,' he thought, 'they could eat it all up. Only I expect Aunt Jen will come and sweep it away. And they aren't here anyway. I wonder if they're terribly hungry?' He sighed heavily, and his father looked across at him.

'Tired, young Fred?' he said, gathering up the sugar bags to check the weight. Tucking up the top of each bag into a pair of neat triangles, he began to stack them away on the shelves. He looked again at Fred over his shoulder. 'Tired?' he repeated. 'Or what?'

There was nobody else in the shop and it was beginning to grow dark. The snow outside was grey. The lamps had not been lit, and a cold twilight lay across the street. Fred sat down on a high stool, and his heels kicked idly against its frame.

'Dad,' he said, 'if a mouse broke its leg would it die?'

Fred's father pushed his hat to the back of his head and stared at the boy before he answered. 'If you know a mouse with a broken leg, you'd best bring it to me. Or to Uncle John. We might fix it. If you're talking about your wooden mouse, I reckon it could be mended with a lick of glue. If it's one of our lot in the cellar, well, I'm not so sure. They're tiny chaps, and delicate. What's the trouble, lad? Still thinking about those traps, are you? I saw to them, you know.'

Words trembled on the end of Fred's tongue and in another moment he would have poured out the whole story; but the shop bell tinkled, and Mrs Bassenthwaite and her little girl came in. Mrs Bassenthwaite had come not only to buy all her stores for the following week but to collect all the local news so that she could pass it on to the rest of the street. Her daughter Lily wandered round the shop, fingering everything within reach. Fred's father gave him a re-signed grin, patted him on the shoulder, and said, 'Off you go, young Fred, and get your tea. Tell your Aunt Jen I won't be long, eh?' So the moment passed. Mrs Bassenthwaite, her glazed eyes fixed on the shelves behind the counter, began a kind of chant to remind herself what she wanted.

'Butter, lard, bacon, eggs, flour,' she intoned. 'Tea, sugar, coffee, cocoa. Treacle, oatmeal. Soap, soda, candles, matches.' Fred slid down from the stool and returned to the kitchen, where Aunt Jen was laying the table and looking accusingly at the clock.

'Hum,' she said. 'I was just coming to see where you'd got to. It's time your Dad came in for his tea. What's he doing now?'

'Mrs Bassenthwaite's come,' said Fred, and Aunt Jen snorted. 'He's stuck, then. Talk the hind leg off a donkey, she would. You sit down there and toast these slices and mind you don't fall in the fire. And don't let them get black.' She passed a plateful of bread to Fred, handed him a toasting fork and pushed him on to a low stool by the fire. Fred sighed. There never seemed to be enough time to sort out his problems. He impaled a slice on the toasting fork and held it close to the glowing coals. He did not understand why it should enter Aunt Jen's head that he should fall in the fire. Indeed it was so hot that he had to lean backwards to stop his face from getting scorched, but he had by now become so used to his aunt's expectation of disaster that he paid little attention. He toasted four slices of bread and passed them over to Aunt Jen to butter. When his father came in from the shop he was finishing the last piece, and his cheeks were rosy from the heat of the fire. Dad rapped him gently on the head on his way to the tea-table.

'That's more like it, lad,' he said as he sat down. 'Got a bit of colour in your face now. I'll be able to tell your Mam you're on the mend. She'll be asking, you know, before I've had time to sit down. "How's young Fred?" she'll say. "All right," I'll say. "Makes toast all right," I'll say. My, I'm ready for it, too.'

He smiled across at Fred, and the boy smiled as he climbed on to his chair and took a bite out of the hot buttery toast. The butter ran down his chin and he wiped it off with the back of his hand. Aunt Jen opened her mouth to reprimand him about his manners, but before she got the words out Fred's father had passed him his own handkerchief and

distracted her attention by asking what he should take to the hospital the next day. After that he turned to his son.

'Did you finish those pictures for Mam?'

Fred said he would finish them after tea, and Aunt Jen said he'd better get on with it because she was going to see that he went to bed early, and Dad said he must go and clear up the shop; and tea ended in a flurry of clearing away and washing up.

Fred wondered what had happened to Alice, and hoped that she would come in soon; but Willie came instead, stamping his feet and blowing on his hands and making his usual commotion. He brought with him little Benjamin, who stood squarely in the middle of the hearthrug and took no notice of anybody. A thick woollen scarf was wound round and round his neck so that his chin rested on its folds, and he was playing with a cup and ball that used to belong to Willie. He was awkward but determined, and kept on trying to catch the ball, talking to himself and giving himself advice in a continuous low mutter. Young Fred sat at the kitchen table colouring his drawing book, his tongue curling round his open mouth as he studied the pictures and carefully made his choice of crayons. Aunt Jen was flitting in and out like an animated feather duster, compulsively brushing and polishing. Willie moved restlessly about the room, occasionally getting under Aunt Jen's feet, and talking all the time.

He dropped on to a chair opposite Fred for a few minutes, put his elbows on the table and his cheeks in his hands, and looked approvingly at Fred's efforts.

'That's all right, Fred. That's really all right. What a lot of grass you've got to do. You'll use all your green up before you've finished, I reckon. So Alice can't come out. My Mam says she's too tired and she's got to go to bed early. Ben's got a cough so he's got to go to bed soon too. Everybody's in bed except me.'

'I'm not,' protested Fred. But Willie went on chattering, getting up from the table and spinning round on his heels.

'– but Alice said to tell you she hasn't forgotten. She's lost her slipper and I said I'd look for it and I did but I can't find it.'

Fred was not at all sure of how much Alice had told Willie about her adventures of the night before, and was at a loss to know how to answer, but fortunately Willie rarely waited for a reply when he was talking, and he rattled on about school and the other children they knew, and the boat Uncle John was making ... 'it's a Noah's Ark for Ben' ...

and kept saying how cold it was. Fred continued to colour his picture, and Ben continued to wrestle with his cup and ball, neither of them paying much attention to Willie who went on talking at random until Aunt Jen went through to the shop 'to tidy up'.

As soon as she had gone Willie said, much more quietly, 'Here, Fred. Alice sent you a stick of licorice. She wrapped it up so it wouldn't get sticky, so don't lose the paper. Here.' He thrust a little packet into Fred's hand, clapped him cheerfully on the shoulder, and made for the kitchen door. Fred started to unwrap the packet, and saw that there was a message printed on the wrapping paper. He stared at Willie with questions written all over his face.

'Time we went home,' Willie said, dragging the door open. 'Come on, Ben.' The next instant he was back again; or at least his head was, poking round the door. 'I say, Fred. When I went by the snow house on the way home from school I smelt a funny smell in it, you know, kind of warm and crumby. I thought we might have lodgers.' He grinned at Fred and flickered his fingers at him, while Fred stared back with his mouth open.

Benjamin gathered up the string and pushed his cup and ball at Fred. 'Your cat caught a mouse,' he said. 'I can't do it, Fred. You do it.' He stood back, stolid and hopeful, and was quite alarmed by Fred's reaction.

'Eh? What did you say? Caught what?'

'She caught a mouse, and it had a stiff leg. Catch my ball, Fred. Catch my ball, *please*. I can't do it.'

Willie came back into the kitchen and stooped down in front of the little boy, putting his hands round Ben's waist. 'Tell us, then, Ben,' he coaxed. 'Tell me, there's a good lad. What did you mean about Puss?'

'She caught a mouse,' repeated Ben, sticking firmly to his guns. 'I heard a noise and I got up to have a look and I saw your cat, Fred. She caught a mouse and she took it home.'

'When, Bennie? What time was it? What day was it?'

'I don't know,' said Ben, confused by so many questions. 'I went to bed and I got up. It wasn't morning yet. Please Fred, can't you catch my ball?'

Fred couldn't, but Willie, who had Uncle John's sure and skilful hands, took the cup and ball from Ben and played tricks with it, not only catching the ball in its wooden bowl but spinning it round on the string half a dozen times before he made it land safely.

'Where's Puss now?' he asked casually as he tossed the ball in and out of the cup, dodging Ben's clutching hands.

'Upstairs in the loft, I expect,' Fred said thoughtfully, amazed at Willie's control of the situation. 'With the kittens. She's mostly there. Did Alice tell you . . . ?' Willie shot a warning glance in Ben's direction, but the little boy was already pursuing a new idea.

'Oh Fred, can I see the kittens?' he began to plead. 'I've never seen the kittens. Dad said I could have a kitten when it's grown. Can I have a kitten, Fred?'

'I tell you what,' said Willie with a wink at Fred, 'I'll go up and fetch one down to show you, eh, Ben?' Before he had finished his sentence he had pushed the cup and ball into Ben's hands and was halfway up the catsteps, and Aunt Jen returned to the kitchen just in time to see his legs disappearing from sight. 'Don't you dare go up there, Ben,' she commanded, seizing him by the seat of his trousers as he set foot on the polished ladder in Willie's wake. 'You'll fall and break all your bones, most likely.'

Ben sat down at the bottom of the catsteps to wait for Willie to come back. In a few minutes his brother reappeared at the top and began to climb down almost as fast as he had gone up. He jumped to the ground, pulled a protesting bundle of black fur out of his pocket, and put it into Ben's arms.

It was like a handful of sparks. Its claws and its fur and

its teeth were needles of fury, and its mouth was wide open to emit a continuous wail. Ben received it with worshipping love, holding it against his chest and patting its bony head with his fat little hand.

Willie rocked for a moment backwards and forwards on his heels, watching his little brother. Then he gently took the kitten from Ben's reluctant arms and passed it over to Fred. 'Come on, Ben,' he said with finality. 'We've got to go home. You can have the kitten when it's bigger. Puss isn't there, Fred. I found our Alice's slipper, though.' He seized Ben firmly by the arm and, pulling the little boy after him, vanished through the doorway with a bang.

'That boy,' said Aunt Jen, 'he does make me jump. I never knew a boy as noisy as he is. And he talks too much. What's that you've got, Fred?'

'Licorice,' said Fred, holding up the black stick he was sucking and keeping the wrapping paper carefully hidden in his hand. 'Alice sent it.'

'H'm,' sniffed Aunt Jen. 'Won't do you any harm, I suppose. Might clear your tubes. Don't swallow it all at once.'

Fred continued to suck thoughtfully at the licorice stick, holding the kitten on his knee. It had lost its belligerence and was settling down into a small soft ball, attempting to purr. Fred tucked under his arm and took it back upstairs to the loft. He put it in the basket with its two brothers who both began to wash it fiercely. There was still no sign of Puss, but when Fred looked behind the basket he saw a small red slipper, half hidden under a heap of empty sugar bags. And there, curled in its toe, lay a mouse, sleeping.

'Almond,' breathed Fred in wonder, 'oh, Almond.'

Almond opened his eyes, stirred, gave Fred a bright look of recognition, and went to sleep again. Fred gazed ecstatically at him, and then remembered Alice's note. He spread it out on the floor and carefully spelt out the pencilled words.

WILLIE WILL GO TO THE SNOW HOUSE
WITH BISCUITS AFTER.

Fred took a long deep breath and sat back on the dusty floor of the loft, leaning against the kittens' basket. So Willie really did know all about everything, and biscuits, he was quite sure, would reach the mice that night. They would not go hungry. Willie would see to it. Tired out with anxiety and his recent illness, Fred found great comfort in his cousin's carefree confidence. As he sat thinking gratefully about Willie, he heard a soft padding footstep and felt the brush of whiskers on his cheek. Puss was beside him, purring loudly. She rubbed her face against his, and jumped into the basket amongst her children, crowing to them as she gathered them close to her. Fred put his hand over the edge of the basket and scratched her ears.

'Puss,' he said, 'are you all right now? You're a wonder, that you are.'

Puss settled herself down and allowed the kittens to climb all over her, washing them each in turn, before she spoke to Fred. 'You have found our young friend, I see. I thought he would be safer up here. He will need some food before long, but he is all right for a while. Perhaps you will bring something for him. And Caradoc must be told.'

'Willie knows he's here,' Fred said. 'He saw Alice's slipper so he must have seen Almond in it because he didn't bring it down. He'll tell Caradoc. Is Almond going to stay here? How did he get here? Did you find him, Puss? How did he get in the slipper?'

Puss described briefly what had happened after Bouncer had been routed. She had waited, crouching in the snow, gathering her strength, until the mice had reached the safety of the snow house. She watched Uncle John come out and rescue Alice, and went on watching until the lights in the bakehouse went out and the Square was in darkness.

Then she crept quietly across the snow and went into the bakehouse to look for Almond.

'But how could you get in?' asked Fred. 'The door was locked.'

'There is always a way in and out if you use your eyes and nose,' said Puss. 'When I had found Almond I brought him here. I went back for the red slipper. It is always important to cover your tracks, and out there in the snow it would have looked like a bright flag. In any case it makes a warm and comfortable bed.'

'Oh Puss, why didn't you tell me before? He's been here all day and I didn't know where he was.' Fred's voice was reproachful.

Puss looked at him, her eyes enormous. 'I believed he would die,' she said. 'It is not easy to talk of such things in your language. But I was mistaken. I watched for a long time without much hope, and I saw his courage coming back as he rested. So I do not have to carry his body to Caradoc, as I had feared. You can take him yourself, alive and well.'

Fred swallowed his tears and looked at Puss, love brimming over in his eyes. 'Ben saw you carrying Almond,' he said slowly. 'He said you'd caught a mouse. But Puss, are you sure the mice are really in the snow house? Alice couldn't hear them this morning.'

'They are there. They will be silent with grief. They don't know yet that Almond is alive. And they will have to move again before long, and make fresh plans. But they need a few days to recover.' Puss got up, shaking off the clinging kittens, and went over to look at Almond. Fred wondered if the kittens could understand their mother's human speech, as they took no notice of it. 'Still sleeping,' said Puss. 'He will soon be well, though I daresay he will always limp a little.'

The shadows in the loft were dark and deep like those in

the cellars. The flickering light of the candle Fred had lit when he brought back the kitten caught the gleam of Puss's eyes and made them shine, black and gold. Young Fred once more felt as though he were living in a strange dream world where he could not tell what was real and what was his own fancy. Puss had stopped speaking, and was purring like any ordinary cat as she looked down at the sleeping mouse curled up in the red slipper. From down below came Aunt Jen's voice, scattering the magic.

'Whatever are you doing up there, young Fred? It's past time you were in bed. Your supper's on the table and your Dad's waiting. Come on down and blow that candle out or we'll have the house on fire.' Disaster was once more threatening Aunt Jen's world.

'Coming, Aunt Jen,' Fred responded dutifully. He blew out the candle and pinched the hot wick in his fingers. 'Good night, Almond,' he whispered. 'Good night, Puss.'

Nobody answered. Fred climbed down the ladder from the loft, and down the catsteps into the kitchen, where the lamp-light and the firelight shone brightly, and only people talked.

[9]

The next day was Saturday. Fred's father left early to catch the train for his visit to the hospital and Mam. Young Fred stood in the doorway watching him go, as he walked down the long snowy street, a carpet bag of gifts in one hand and a bunch of red roses in the other. Fred's book of pictures, wrapped up in brown paper, was wedged under his arm. He turned when he reached the corner, and Fred waved both arms at him, shouting at the top of his voice, 'Give my love to Mam.' His father was out of earshot, but he waved the bunch of red roses cheerfully in response to Fred's gesture as he disappeared round the corner. For a moment, as he stood staring after his father, a great cloud of loneliness and longing descended on Fred; but Aunt Jen shuffled him briskly back into the kitchen for his breakfast. She had planned what she called 'a good clean through' while Dad was away, so mercifully Fred was to be allowed out.

As soon as he had finished his breakfast he went back upstairs, muttering in answer to Aunt Jen's inquiry something about fetching apples to take out with him. He went straight up to the loft. Puss met him at the top of the ladder, purring musically in greeting. The kittens in the basket were squealing and crowing and spitting as they played, boxing each other, needling each other with their tiny claws and nipping each other's ears with their sharp little teeth. Fred thrust his hand in amongst them and they all fell to biting and scratching him, wriggling in delight as he caressed their soft little bodies. He detached himself from their clutching claws and tiptoed across the creaking boards to peep into Alice's slipper.

It was empty. Fred's heart missed a beat, but the next instant he heard a squeak from the top of an old chest in the far corner, and there, to his joy, was Almond, sitting up bright-eyed among the cobwebs, cleaning his whiskers. Fred stretched out a hand to him, and the mouse moved slowly forward to the edge of the chest. Though the splint that Uncle John had put on his leg made him walk stiffly, with a slight limp, he seemed quite lively. Fred did not say a word, but sat back on his heels and waited. Puss, stepping delicately over the empty boxes that were heaped higgledy-piggledy in the loft, reached Almond's side with an easy leap on to the chest. Murmuring in his ear, she picked him up in her mouth, jumped down from the chest, and dropped the mouse on the floor beside Fred's knee. Almond shook himself and looked up at the boy. Fred picked him up, enfolded him carefully in his handkerchief, and tucked him into his jacket pocket. Puss, purring in approval, rubbed her face against Fred's chin. Then she slid away from him and went back into the basket, where she lay down with the kittens climbing all over her in an ecstasy of welcome.

Young Fred had learnt a lot in the last few days, and they all seemed to understand each other though not a word had been spoken, at least in human language. He got slowly to his feet, leaned over the basket and scratched Puss behind her ear. She licked his finger, stretched out her neck, closed her eyes, and purred. Fred, with Almond safely in his pocket, climbed down the catsteps. He was taking Almond back to his own people.

In the kitchen Aunt Jen was already prepared for her on-slaught on the dust and dirt that she was convinced lurked all over the house. The chairs were upside down on the table and all the rugs were rolled up. An armoury of buckets and mops and brushes were arrayed in battle order on the floor, and the smell of soapsuds hung heavily on the air. Fred did not have to waste any time. Muffled up to his eyebrows, he stuffed his coat pockets with little apples and raced away across the Square, pursued by Aunt Jen's dire warnings about what would happen if he caught cold again. He reached the snow house and crouched eagerly beside it, his mouth against one of the windows. The frozen snow burnt his lips, and his breath rose like a plume of smoke as he called to the mice inside.

'Caradoc,' he cried. 'Oh Caradoc, Sir. Almond's all right, at least he nearly is. Caradoc, are you there, Caradoc? Have you got Singleton and all the others?' He stopped and listened, but could hear nothing. He pulled the apples out of his pockets and posted them through the windows of the snow house. They dropped with a series of muffled thumps, and once more Fred listened intently, but there was no sound and no movement. Panic shook him. He knelt down in the snow and pushed his face into the doorway, trying to penetrate the darkness inside. 'Caradoc,' he whispered, desperately. 'Please, Caradoc. I've brought Almond back, Sir.'

There was a sudden rustle in the darkness of the snow house. A tiny cold claw touched Fred's nose, making him start back. Bright eyes gleamed at every window, and the silence that had been so awful and absolute was shattered by a chorus of excited squeaks. There in the doorway, framed by the sparkling snow, crouched Caradoc. And in Fred's jacket pocket there was suddenly a minor eruption.

Fred's cold fingers tore at his buttons, dragged open his coat and pulled out the handkerchief from which Almond was struggling to free himself. He released the mouse from its folds and put him on the ground face to face with Caradoc. The two small creatures crouched for a moment in silence, without moving; then their noses met in greeting and recognition, and Fred turned his head away, not wishing to intrude.

Squeaks from the doorway recalled him. Caradoc and Almond sat side by side, their tails erect. Caradoc bowed his head in Fred's direction, then in one quick movement vanished into the snow house. Almond limped slowly after him. Fred called out softly, 'Don't worry. I'll be coming back,' and jumping to his feet, ran joyfully to the bakehouse.

Uncle John was busy with an order for a winter wedding and the bakery smelt richly of fruit cake and mincemeat and pies. The biggest oven was already full of steak puddings, bone broth and joints that had been brought in by people who lived nearby to be cooked for the next day, and would be carried, steaming, across the Square on Sunday morning. Alice and Willie and Fred, supplied by Auntie Patty with hot muffins, assembled in the kitchen for a council of war. Ben, busy on the floor trying to mend the stirrups on his

74

spotted horse, talked to himself and seemed to be ignoring the conversation.

Fred told them all about the safe return of Almond to the snow house, and promised to bring back Alice's slipper which he had forgotten about in the excitement. Alice was in transports of delight at the prospect of looking after a tribe of mice who could talk, and embarked on a recital of what she thought they would like to eat, day by day.

'Porridge,' she said, licking her pencil as she wrote out the list. 'And biscuits. Apples and cakes and buns and cheese. Bacon rinds – do they like bacon, Fred?' she frowned, concentrating on bringing an attractive variety into the diet of their lodgers. Fred was irresistibly reminded of Mrs Bassenthwaite reciting her shopping list. He thought they should set a guard on the snow house in case any unknown enemies should attack its occupants, but this seemed to be too difficult because, as Willie pointed out, they would all be at school except Ben, and he was not old enough to be responsible.

'We can keep looking in at them, though, when we come home,' said Fred, 'and Puss will look after them as well. Puss says they have to go somewhere else soon, but I wish they wouldn't.'

Willie, who had been sitting still for quite five minutes, chained to the table by his muffin, got up and began to prowl about the room. 'Well, we'd have to think of somewhere for them to go later anyway,' he said, his hands deep in his pockets. 'They can't stay in the snow house forever, can they?'

'I don't see why they can't,' said Alice, pushing her hair out of her eyes. 'Nobody else wants it, only us, and it's ours, isn't it?'

'But it won't go on being there,' said Willie. 'One of these days it's going to melt, and whoosh – there they'll all go in the flood. We'll have to move them before that.'

'Then we'll get a boat,' said Alice definitely, dismissing the subject. She went over to see what Ben was doing on the floor, and put an end to the conversation. Fred frowned. He had grown so accustomed to the snow that he had quite forgotten the possibility of its disappearing, and was filled with alarm at the thought. Ben was still talking away to himself.

'If I put it this way it won't keep on,' he told himself, 'but if you put it that way it might do it. Stand still, Dobbin. How can I do it for you if you don't stand still?' He looked up at Alice. 'I don't want my snow house to go away.'

Willie squatted down beside him, took the stirrup and began to fix it on to the horse's saddle. 'Don't worry, Ben. It won't go away for a long time yet. There. Old Dobbin's stirrup's fixed. Shall I make him a stable with these chairs so he can go inside to bed?'

'No, no!' shouted Ben. 'Make him a boat, Willie. Make a boat and I'll put Dobbin in it. And my pigs. And my cows and sheep and little horses. They can all go sailing on the water ...' Ben started to sail about the room himself, holding out his arms like wings. Willie swooped after him and rolled him over and over on the rug until he almost choked with laughter. Fred and Alice began to laugh too, and Willie suddenly pulled Ben to his feet and stuffed him into his coat.

'Come on out,' he said, pulling on his own coat, and seizing his little brother by the hand he hurled them both out into the Square. 'Come on!' he shouted back at the others. 'Let's go and make snowballs.'

Willie's enthusiasm was infectious. Alice and Fred followed him out, and in a few minutes they were all racing and sliding about, pelting each other with snowballs. Ben kept falling over and getting up again, gasping with laughter as he tried unsuccessfully to fend off the snowballs that were flung at him. At last Alice pulled him up by the ends of his scarf and rubbed her cold rosy cheek against his.

'Come on, lad. There's snow down your neck and look at your hands – they're purple. Mam'll be mad at us.' She rubbed Ben's swollen fingers to warm them, and pulled his woollen cap down over his ears. Willie was still shouting joyously, tossing handfuls of loose snow into the air and capering round like a foal. Auntie Patty appeared in the doorway, calling them in; so in they went, beating the snow off their coats, the mice and their problems forgotten.

Fred spent the whole day with his cousins – a long happy day. Uncle John bustled in and out, full of merriment. Auntie Patty left the children alone to enjoy their Saturday, only intervening to provide meals and warmth and comfort. At tea-time Fred thought sadly of Aunt Jen in The Sundial, scrubbing and scouring the flavour out of the house. Alice said, 'Fred could take a teacake and some curranty home with him, couldn't he, Mam?'

Auntie Patty stared at her in astonishment. 'Indeed he could not,' she said very firmly. 'I wouldn't be so rude to Aunt Jen. She's a good cook and my teacakes are no better than hers. She might be insulted, and quite right too. Whatever next, I wonder? What are you thinking about, Alice?'

Alice, who had only been thinking about provisions for the mice, could not explain herself, but blushed and hung her head. Fred did not know what to say. Uncle John, with a quick look at the children, came to the rescue.

'Our Fred has always gone for your curranty, Patty, and it's your Gran's old recipe. I daresay if young Fred took him a present it wouldn't come amiss.'

Auntie Patty looked uncertain, and Fred said, 'Just a small piece, please, Auntie Patty. I'll give it to Aunt Jen. She likes it too.'

Alice and Fred exchanged glances full of guilt, knowing full well that neither Fred's father nor Aunt Jen would ever see a crumb of whatever Auntie Patty might provide. A small parcel of curranty and a couple of fresh teacakes was accordingly wrapped up for Fred to take home, and with it tucked into his pocket he set off towards The Sundial. The Square was lit by a lamp at each corner, and Fred's shadow danced before him as he trotted across the snow.

He stopped at the snow house, unwrapped the parcel, broke up its contents and scattered the crumbs through the windows. Crushing the paper into a ball and pushing it back into his pocket, he stooped to speak to the mice inside the little fortress. 'It's all right,' he whispered. 'Don't you worry. We'll look after you, Alice and Willie and me. You'll be all right.'

Inside the snow house nothing stirred. The snow was blue in the lamplight, the air was as sharp and frosty as ever, the ground underfoot was crisp and hard, and large flakes of snow fell aimlessly, touching Fred's cheeks with a cold soft caress. There was no sign of a break in the weather. Winter still governed the world, and as far as Fred could tell, it always would.

Dad was already home when young Fred reached The Sundial; sitting by the fire with his feet in the hearth, while the kettle whispered and spluttered on the hob.

'Well, young Stay-away,' he called across the kitchen. 'Better late than never. Thought you'd left home for good. Mam sent her love. She's up and about and talking about coming home in the spring. What about that, then? She liked your picture book. She's got it by her bed on the table so she can keep looking at it. Here. She sent you a present.'

Fred took the parcel his father handed to him, unwrapped it, and spread the contents all over the hearthrug. There was a box of coloured pencils and a little pocket knife to sharpen them with. Aunt Jen opened her mouth to utter warnings about cut fingers, but shut it again as Dad shook his head at her. There was a packet of humbugs, a square white india rubber with black printing on it, and a new drawing book;

and wrapped in tissue-paper, a little brightly dressed clown on a ladder that turned somersaults when Fred squeezed the sides. And there was a letter.

'Dear Fred,' it said. 'Love from Mam.'

Young Fred sat on the rug and listened while his father told him all about the hospital and Mam. For once Aunt Jen did not interrupt, but sat quietly listening too.

'When's she coming home then?' asked Fred, fingering the letter from his mother.

'Ah well – not for a few weeks yet,' said Dad. 'She's got to get a bit stronger yet. She's still got a bit of a patch, you see.' Fred imagined the kind of patch Aunt Jen stitched on to his trousers, and wondered wherever it could have been sewn on Mam. 'But it won't be long – and I can go now every week to see her.' His voice was quiet, as he saw his wife's face, now so far away. Then he looked down at Fred and smiled. 'When the snow's gone, maybe.'

When the snow's gone. Young Fred began to think again about the mice and what Willie had said about the snow house not being there forever. 'But it must be there,' he thought to himself. 'It's big and strong and hard and Uncle John made it. It can't go away. It will always be there, always.'

'Whey-hey, Young Fred,' said his father, looking into his son's solemn blue eyes. 'What are you dreaming about now, eh? Come on back. It won't be long before Mam's home.' He grinned at Fred and poked his finger into his ribs. Waving his pipe at Aunt Jen, he said, 'Supper-time, isn't it? I'm as empty as a barrel full of air. Let's have it by the fire.'

10

So the bright days went by. January was nearly over, and the white winter went on and on. Fresh falls of snow covered the ground, laying a soft new carpet every day until it was trodden hard by the children's feet. And in the Square the snow house sparkled still.

Every evening after tea, when the lamps were lit and a strange blue radiance shone upon the snow, Fred and Alice and Willie went to play with the mice. They waited until Ben had gone to bed. He was not old enough, Alice thought, to be trusted with secrets, and he did not take part in their games. He could keep his own counsel, all the same. He never saw the mice, who only came out after dark; but he knew they were there, hidden away in the magic and mystery of the snow house. He often played there by himself while the others were at school, and he sang to them as he trotted about on the slippery snow. 'Mouses, mouses, come out of your houses,' he chanted; but they never did, and as Ben was in the habit of talking to himself, nobody who heard him took any notice.

The mice soon learnt to expect the children, and would appear at the windows and in the doorway, taking cheese from their fingers. Some even grew bold enough to come outside and scamper up and down the carriage drive, picking up the crumbs that were scattered for them; and they would climb out through the windows and scramble all over the roof, clinging on with sharp claws, their whiskers powdery with snow. The children were enchanted, and brought so much food for them to eat that the mice grew fat.

Fred longed to see Caradoc and Almond, and most of all little Singleton, but for some reason they never emerged from the snow house, and though Fred always called to them by name, they did not answer. He began to wonder if they had forgotten how to talk. Even Puss seemed to avoid his company nowadays. When he went up to play with the kittens in the loft she purred at him as she had always done, but she did not answer when he talked to her about the mice, though he was sure she visited them because he had seen her footprints in the snow. So he continued to play happily with his friends in the snow house, and to feast them on the choicest titbits he could find.

*

The truth was that both Caradoc and Puss were desperately worried by the turn things had taken. The easy life, the security, the unending supply of rich food, and the attentions of the children, had changed the natures of the mice. They had lost their shy alertness, and their awareness of danger was fast disappearing. They were becoming idle and contented. Only a few of them remained wary.

'We're too comfortable by half,' said Almond to Arthington as they crouched together in the snow house, away from the others. 'Nobody has to search for food any more. Nobody has to lift a claw to help himself. We're all getting lazy.'

'And far too friendly, if you ask me,' agreed Arthington. 'Look at that Otley crowd, now. They're all sitting by the windows waiting to be fed like pets in a cage. It won't do us any good. There's only you and me and Janus, and Caradoc of course, who've kept our wits about us. The others seem to have taken leave of their senses.'

Almond looked round the snow house. 'It's the children I'm worried about,' he said. 'It's no way to bring up children. Singleton's all right. He does what Caradoc tells him. And the Cleveland-Tontines, they're wary enough and never go out showing off. But the others ... well, it's better than traps and starvation, I suppose.'

81

'I'm not so sure,' said Arthington morosely. 'I doubt if anybody would recognize a trap now. And look at the size of those young ones – as round as brandy-balls, they are.

'We'd better talk to Caradoc,' said Almond decisively. 'Come on.'

They scampered together across to the other side of the snow house where Caradoc sat alone. Almond's damaged leg had mended, and though he dragged it a little he could still move very swiftly.

'Caradoc, Sir,' he began, 'how much longer are we going to stay here?'

The two mice spoke earnestly about their anxiety, appealing to their leader for help and advice, and the old mouse listened gravely.

'I, too, am deeply concerned,' he replied, and added a dignified reproof. 'Do you suppose that I have forgotten the welfare of my people? I am as troubled as you are. This timely refuge, provided by our friends in an hour of need, was never intended to serve as a permanent home.' Arthington stirred restlessly as Caradoc's sonorous phrases rolled slowly out, and Almond had to restrain his impetuous friend with a warning look. Caradoc might be old, and perhaps a little pompous, but he was wise and noble and was in no way to be trifled with. Arthington subsided, and Caradoc went on. 'Events, however, have overtaken us. We urgently need to take council together. But,' he lifted his grey muzzle and looked across at the mice clustered round the windows, 'for the first time in my life, I confess, I am uncertain of the loyalty of the tribe. We should plan to travel elsewhere; but I fear I may have difficulty in leading my people away from here. They have become accustomed to luxury and do not wish to give it up. I have spoken on several occasions of the need for caution and the advisability of considering our departure, and I have been conscious of a feeling of ... of rebellion in the tribe.'

'Rebellion!' exclaimed Arthington. 'I'd give them rebellion. That's Calverley's lot, I'll be bound.' He jumped high into the air in indignation, but Caradoc raised a restraining paw and he sat down again, muttering under his breath. Caradoc looked pacifically at him, and went on. 'The Otleys are young and foolish and have much to learn, but this life of idleness is destroying the common sense of many others too. If it continues long, I fear for our survival. They grow careless, all of them. Carelessness spells danger. And I am afraid.'

He paused, and Almond, seeing his distress, spoke quietly and respectfully.

'What, Sir, must we do then?'

Caradoc did not reply at once, but let his eyes rove round the snow house over the groups of well-fed mice.

'Forgive me,' he said at last; 'I was counting my possible allies. You ask me what we shall do. For the present, nothing. Only be very watchful, and wait. I have talked with Puss, and this is her advice. Wait, she says, for a change in the weather, which her senses tell her will not be long. Our people's memories are very short, as you know, and they need a sharp reminder of danger; sharper than any words of mine can be – or yours, my friends,' with a quizzical look at Arthington. 'When the weather breaks this house will fall, and we shall have to act quickly. It is a desperate and dangerous remedy, but things have gone so far that it is our only hope. And at least, in extremity, we shall be united and the tribe will be held together. At all costs our people must not be scattered. So have patience, my loyal friends. Who knows ...' In spite of their fears, Almond and Arthington began to smile. They knew what was coming next. It was what Caradoc always said when he was quietly exerting his authority. 'Who knows what tomorrow may bring?'

It was also his signal that the conversation was at an end.

11

As things turned out the desperate and dangerous remedy that Caradoc had foretold came much sooner than he expected, and had nothing to do with the weather. The life of idle luxury the mice were enjoying came to a sudden end, and it was Benjamin who had to report, as best he could, the events of that dreadful February afternoon.

The other children, Willie and Alice and Fred, were all at school. Ben was lonely and bored and longed for company; and after dinner he wandered off into the Square vaguely hoping for some friends to play with. There was nobody about: only an empty crisp expanse of snow, with shut-eyed houses on all three sides, and the snow house in the middle shining like a crystal dome. It was half-day closing, and even the bakehouse and The Sundial were shut. The little boy ran about for a while, talking to himself and rubbing his hands together to keep warm.

'Don't you stay out too long,' called Auntie Patty from the bakehouse door. 'I'll have a hot pancake for you when Alice and Willie come home.'

Ben waved his mittens and slid across the snow. It was then that he saw the man, coming round the corner at the far end of the Square, past The Sundial kitchen door. He was a smallish man in a long heavy coat that came right down to his boots, with a rope tied round it for a belt and a grey woollen scarf tucked into its collar. He had a battered and crumpled top hat on his head, and thick grey mittens on his hands. There was a small square cart that looked like a box on two wheels, covered with black tarpaulin, and the man was pulling it behind him, like an old horse between the shafts. A thin black dog with a matted tangled tail trot-

ted at the back of the cart between the wheels, and two
skittish white donkeys, tethered loosely to the cart, followed
jauntily along, side by side.

Ben, stopped in his tracks by this remarkable sight, opened
his mouth and stared. The man turned his head, saw the

little boy standing by the snowball and came across the Square towards him. The donkeys shook their shaggy heads as they suddenly had to change direction, and the dog crouched closer to the ground. Ben shrank away as the strange group approached. The man's chin was dark blue and bristly, his thick black eyebrows stuck out under the broken brim of his hat, his bulbous eyes rolled round and round, and he had a lumpy nose much too big for his face. His back looked humped and bent when he was pulling his cart, and he had to turn his face up sideways to look at Ben. When he came close he stopped, set down the shafts, and stood up, clapping his hands together and blowing on his fingers, while the dog crept forward, growling softly and sniffing round the toes of the man's enormous boots. The donkeys frisked in the snow, kicking it up in a little misty cloud with their delicate hoofs.

'Now then, young gentleman,' said the man, 'would you be living round about?'

Ben opened his mouth and gulped, but did not answer. His eyes travelled over the dancing donkeys, the black cart, and the questing dog. The man spoke to him again.

'Jem Leary,' he said, patting his chest and grinning at Ben. 'Jem Leary, Mouse Circus. Two thirty and six thirty, shilling a time, children half price. You ask your Mammy and your Daddy to bring you now, won't you? Tomorrow afternoon on the Council Field. Donkey rides after the show, threepence a go. My feet,' he added in a mournful tone, 'my feet are killing me. Tell me now, young gentleman, how far would it be to the Council Field from here?'

The words 'Mouse Circus' fascinated Ben, and the cheerful donkeys gave him confidence enough to reply. 'It's over there,' he said, waving vaguely in the right direction. 'It's called the Sally Lunn. What's a mouse circus? Where is it?'

The little man slapped the black tarpaulin cover. 'It's all in here, young gentleman. All in here, see?' He pointed to some large white letters painted on the cart. Ben could not read, so the man spelt them out for him. M-O-U-S-E mouse,' he said in his curious husky voice. 'C-I-R-C-U-S. That's for circus. Mouse Circus. Dancing mice, fighting mice, mice playing in a band. Never seen anything like it. Shilling a time. I'm running a bit short, though. They don't last long.' He gave a harsh grating laugh. 'Seen any mice round here, young gentleman? I pay good money, penny for each mouse and a balloon for free. Trust Jem Leary.'

Ben was suddenly afraid. He backed farther and farther away from the man with the rolling eyes and the leering grin. The dog followed him, its nose to the ground, trembling with excitement. Suddenly it leapt beyond him and reared itself up against the crystal wall of the snow house, whining and barking ecstatically.

'What's to do then, Bullseye boy?' growled the man. 'Come back here. There's no mice there.' He stopped, listened, and started to sniff, horribly like his dog. 'There can't be ... but I've never known him wrong yet. Let's have a look-o.'

Ben, terrified, spread himself against the snowball and started to chatter wildly. 'No, no,' he shouted. 'It's our snow house. It's Willie's and mine and Fred's and Alice's. You can't ... you can't ... but the dog was jumping and barking all round him, and the man came closer and closer, sniffing eagerly.

'Mice, mice,' muttered the man. 'I can smell mice right enough. There can't be ... but what a find, eh?' He was close to the snowball now, his rolling eyes scanning the windows. He was on his knees, peering through the doorway. From somewhere about his person he took a little lump of cheese with a piece of dirty thread tied round it, and proceeded to dangle it outside the snow house windows like a conker on a string. The next moment Ben saw the mice for the first time. Small pointed faces appeared, whiskers trembling, round eyes gleaming eagerly at the sight of the swinging cheese, and half a dozen mice were climbing out to reach it.

'Ha, ha, ha !' cried the man. The dog barked wildly, and too late the foolhardy mice realized their danger. They fled in terror back into the recesses of the snow house. Then to Ben's horror the man extracted from the inside of his huge coat a long stick with a dreadful kind of mechanical hand on the end of it. He thrust it through one of the windows, poked it about, and drew it out again with a shout of triumph.

'There's mice – there's really mice, Bullseye boy,' he chortled, looking at the little creature struggling in the vice of the catching stick. 'Oh what a find, eh?' From a pocket in his coat he pulled a large canvas bag and dropped the mouse into it. Ben shrieked in protest, beating the man with his feet and fists, while the dog growled and snarled round his legs.

'Now, young gentleman,' the man was gasping in excitement and irritation. 'Don't you spoil my trade. Leave him alone, Bullseye. We don't want no trouble. Just you let be, young gentleman, and let your Mammy bring you to the circus. You'll have a lovely show, I tell you straight. Trust Jem Leary.' All this time the man was fending off Ben's unavailing attacks, and collecting mice from the snow house, one after another, and dropping them into the canvas bag. It was a nightmare for poor Ben that seemed to go on forever. But at last the man drew back.

'No more, I reckon,' he said, grinning happily. 'What a find eh? Here, young gentleman, I tell you what. You shall have a balloon for free. Always trust Jem Leary.' He dived once more into his overcoat pocket, pulled out a red balloon, blew it up, tied it with string and thrust it into Ben's hand. 'There you are, young gentleman. We'll be getting along. Don't forget to ask your Mammy. Tomorrow at the Council

88

Field. Two thirty and six thirty. Come on, Bullseye.' He flung the dreadful bag full of captured mice into the black cart, picked up the shafts and trundled off, followed by his dog and his donkeys; and Benjamin was left sitting in the snow, clutching his bright red balloon and sobbing bitterly.

It was there that Willie and Alice found him when they came home from school. The smell of Auntie Patty's pancakes and hot treacle was floating across the Square, making the children's throats swell with hunger, but Fred had to turn off at the corner and go home to Aunt Jen's bread and jam. Alice and Willie were skittering towards the bakehouse when they came upon the desolate and bedraggled little boy, weeping in the snow. Alice put both arms round him and held him tight.

'It's all right, Ben, it's all right. Me and Willie are here. What's the matter, love? What's wrong, Ben?'

'A man came,' sobbed Ben, struggling to his knees and clutching Alice. 'He came and he put his hands in the snow house and he took all the mouses and put them in a big black box with wheels on. There was a long thin dog like a hoop and two donkeys. They were nice, the donkeys. The man was awful . . .' Tears ran down his cheeks and down his cold red nose. Willie whirled away to explore the snow house, and the silence inside it confirmed Ben's story.

Alice continued to comfort the little boy as best she could, gently prompting him with questions to which he managed to reply through his sobs; and gradually she and Willie built up a picture of what had happened. They all crouched together in the snow, staring at one another, not knowing what to do next. Ben gulped, and began to cry again quietly to himself as he remembered the little mice struggling in the grip of the catching stick. Willie, looking round at the cold empty Square and the deserted snow house, as the light began to fade, muttered desperately, 'What'll we do now? Whatever can we do?'

Alice jumped to her feet and heaved Ben up from his knees. 'Tell Fred,' she announced firmly. She seized Ben's hand, shook the powdery snow off her skirt, and set off towards The Sundial. Willie hesitated. He turned back to the snow house and once more peered into its dark interior in a wild hope that Ben might have been wrong; but nothing was stirring. Only the faint smell that had betrayed the presence of the mice still lingered. Willie raced after Alice and Ben, and caught them up outside The Sundial door. He pulled urgently at Alice's sleeve. 'We can't tell Fred anything in there. Everybody will know about the mice and you said it was a secret.'

'Don't be silly,' said Alice. 'Of course we won't tell him in there. We're going to get him for tea.' She looked at Ben's tear-stained face, and thrust his hand into Willie's. 'You two stay outside,' she said, 'and I'll get Fred.' With a final pat on the top of Ben's head she turned on her heel, and opening The Sundial door, skipped into the kitchen.

Tea was almost ready. Fred's father was sitting at the table and young Fred was standing on one leg beside him, leaning on the arm of his chair and showing him his school book. Aunt Jen was slicing away at a large loaf of bread which she clasped against her chest, and the big iron kettle was hissing and bubbling on the hob. They all looked up as the door opened.

'Now, young Alice,' said Fred's father with a broad smile of welcome, 'haven't you got a kiss for your uncle?' Alice tripped across to him. He gave her a great hug, and as he released her he gently curled his fingers in the strands of her dark hair. Young Fred looked surprised. It was less than half an hour since they had come from school together and he thought she had gone home. Aunt Jen sniffed.

'Tea's just about ready,' she said, and went on cutting up the loaf. Alice spoke to her uncle.

'Can Fred have his tea in our house?' she said, jigging

from one foot to the other. 'Can he? We've got something to show him.'

Aunt Jen set down the loaf in exasperation. The casual comings and goings of the children were a constant trial to her orderly mind, and she could never get used to their haphazard way of eating meals in each other's houses without any prearrangement. Not that Fred's cousins had been to The Sundial for many meals since Mam had been away. It was not that Aunt Jen begrudged them food, but she liked to know well in advance if they were coming. Their spontaneous arrival would throw her into such a flutter of agitation that they had got out of the habit of drifting in and out as they used to do. She frowned at Alice over her spectacles.

'I don't know,' she said. 'I really don't know. Here's young Fred's tea just ready and in you come like a bombshell taking him away.' She slapped the loaf with the bread knife, and turning to Fred's father, appealed to him crossly for support.

He looked ruefully at her offended expression, and then into Alice's troubled eyes, and with his usual sensitive sympathy came to the rescue. Drawing his chair up to the table and settling his hat firmly on his head, he said in a voice of quiet authority, 'All right, Jen. You and I will eat up all Fred's tea while he goes gallivanting. Off you go, lad. And don't be late back. Your uncle will see you home, I daresay.' He gave Fred a friendly push, raised his eyebrows at Alice, and nodded at Aunt Jen. Alice smiled gratefully at him, Fred struggled into his coat, and they ran off together, followed by Aunt Jen's disapproving glare. They heard her say severely 'You're too soft with that boy, Fred. Too soft by half.'

'Ah, Jen, let them be. They're living in their own world. It won't be long before they all grow up and their playing days will be over and done with. Let them be for now.' Out in the snow with Willie and Ben, Fred and Alice did not hear his answer. In any case there were more important things to think of.

They all trudged across the Square, Alice holding Ben's hand, while she and Willie between them told Fred the terrible story and Ben uttered a series of small gulping sobs. Fred was overcome with horror and grief. He wanted to stop at the snow house, but 'It's no good, Fred,' Willie said. 'There's nobody there. I've tried.' So they went sadly on, Fred asking question after question, which Willie answered as well as he could, for Ben was unable to say a word. It was almost dark. Lights in the bakehouse windows shone warm and welcoming and made gold patches on the snow, but before they went indoors Alice stopped to scrub at Ben's face with her handkerchief.

'Now you musn't cry any more, Bennie. And you musn't tell Mam and Dad about the mice. It's a secret, see? We're going to find them, Willie and Fred and me. Don't you forget, now. Come on in and have your tea.'

Young Fred, near to tears himself, said mournfully, 'I don't reckon we'll ever find them, though. They've gone, Alice. They may be dead. We don't know where they are.'

Alice tossed her head and gave a little jump of impatience. 'Yes we do so. 'They're on the Sally Lunn, aren't they? In the Mouse Circus, Ben said. We'll get them out. So come on in.' She clicked up the latch of the bakehouse door and let out a flood of light and the rich smell of hot pancakes into the darkening street. Bouncing into the kitchen, she flung off her cap and spun Ben round and round as she pulled off his long woollen scarf. The others followed her in, as Ben gave a last gulping sob.

'You're late coming in,' said Auntie Patty as she carried a pile of plates from the warm hearth, wrapped in a cloth. 'What's the matter with Ben? What are you crying for, lad?'

'He fell over in the snow and bumped his nose a bit,' Alice invented cheerfully, 'and he was a bit cold, too, I reckon. You're all right now, aren't you, Ben?' Ben nodded without looking up, and Alice, taking his coat off for him and rubbing his chilled hands, went on 'He wants his tea, don't you, Ben?' She lifted him on to his chair and took off her own coat. 'Fred's come for his tea and all.'

'I can see he has,' said Auntie Patty, 'so you'd better get another plate out of the cupboard and put it down to warm. Take your coat off, lad. Willie, your coat goes on the hook and not on the floor. Mind your fingers, Ben. Sit down, Fred. Sit down, Willie, do. You make a draught all over the place.'

The cheerful chatter went on. Auntie Patty's pancakes were piping hot and running over with dark brown treacle. The glowing fire murmured quietly to itself, and in spite of his grief Fred felt warmed and comforted. He ate five pancakes and sat back, sticky and full.

'You'll burst, young Fred,' said Uncle John, coming in with flour on his chin. 'Anything left for me, Mam?'

'Dad,' said Willie with his mouth full of pancake, 'there's a circus on the Sally Lunn. Can we go?'

'Circus? First I've heard of it. There was a circus there before Christmas, but it's gone long since. There'll be no circus there now, lad.' Uncle John sat down at the table and helped himself to pancakes while Auntie Patty poured his tea.

'There is, Dad. It's different. It's a Mouse Circus. Can we go, Dad?'

Uncle John laughed as he poured treacle all over his plate. 'Whoever heard of a mouse circus?' he mocked at Willie, and picked up his cup of tea. 'Somebody's been telling you fairy tales. Our Alice, I reckon. She's always telling stories about mice, is Alice.'

Ben looked up and opened his mouth, but Alice answered

in a hurry before he could say anything. 'It wasn't me,' she said, with a great show of false indignation. 'They told us at school, didn't they, Willie? It's tomorrow, I think.' She gazed innocently at her father and Fred was astonished at such duplicity. So was Ben, and he stared at Alice with wide eyes, but Willie rallied bravely to her support. 'That's right,' he said. 'Friday. I don't know what time.'

This was true enough. Poor Ben had only been able to tell them half of what the man had said, and there was a great deal more they would have to find out for themselves. To their surprise Auntie Patty supplied quite a lot of information.

'There's treacle all down your chin, Willie. Wipe it up or it will be on your jacket. There is some kind of a circus on the Sally Lunn,' she added, pouring more tea for herself and more milk for Fred. 'Harry Barker came in with the cream and he was talking about it. There's a paper in the post office window, he said. I wasn't taking much notice, but now I come to think of it he did say something about performing mice. And donkeys, he said. He'd seen them walking through the town.'

'Well, that's something I've never seen yet,' said Uncle John. 'Performing fleas, yes; but mice ... On the Sally Lunn, is it? My, it'll be cold up there this weather.'

The Sally Lunn was the name by which the Council Field had been known affectionately to the people of the town as long as anybody could remember. Although the field had been levelled as far as possible, it was still curved enough to rise in the middle and slope slightly downhill towards the edges, like a large tea-cake. It was the despair of visiting cricket teams who found it unnerving to lose sight of a fast bowler as he disappeared over the horizon to start his run; but the locals knew its hazards, and many a match was won not by merit, but by the allowances they made for the shape of the ground.

'Can we go, Dad?' Alice pleated the tablecloth in her fingers and looked appealingly at her father. 'Fred could come and all. Willie and me would look after Ben.'

'We'll see,' her mother said. And with that the children had to be content for the time being. They played together in the kitchen after tea, and Alice read to Ben to keep him happy. When Auntie Patty had taken him upstairs to put him to bed, the other three had half an hour before Fred had to go home; no mice in the snow house to play with; and feeling very desolate, they tried to work out a plan of rescuing them from the circus man.

'We'll have to find out where he keeps them, and then go back after the circus and get them out,' said Willie, walking restlessly up and down the kitchen.

'But we'll have to tell them we're coming,' Fred said. 'They'll all be so frightened and they'll have to know we're coming for them. If only we could find Caradoc he'd tell them what to do.'

'I tell you what,' said Alice in her usual decisive way, 'we'll have to go twice. First time we'll tell them and next day we'll get them.'

Fred, appalled at the thought of leaving his friends in the hands of the circus man for two whole days, pleaded desperately, 'Can't we get them tomorrow? Can't we bring them back? Willie said to go back after the circus and get them, Alice.'

Alice shook her head. 'We can't,' she said. 'How can we? There's that dog for a start. He'd hear us and start barking and wake everybody up and the man would come out and see us. Ben said there's donkey rides. Ben and Willie can have donkey rides with everybody else, and talk to the man, while Fred and me go round the back and get the mice. They know us better,' she added in a lordly tone, 'and they'll talk to Fred. You'll have to keep on with the donkeys till you see we've gone, Willie. And we can't get them tomorrow because there's another circus the next day, but the man will be going on Saturday night, I reckon, and he won't be looking for his mice till after he gets there. And we've got to go to school tomorrow so we can't even go looking till after tea.' After this long and breathless speech, which made Fred quite bemused, Alice pushed her hair out of her eyes and jumped to her feet as her mother came downstairs. 'Mam,' she went on, 'if there's a circus tomorrow it will be after tea, won't it? Everybody will be at school till after tea.'

'I daresay,' said Auntie Patty, going over to the pantry, 'but tomorrow is tomorrow and not tonight.' She poured milk into a saucepan and set it on the fire. She put three mugs on the table and spooned a generous helping of brown sugar into each one. Standing by the fire, waiting for the milk to warm, she smiled at the children and thought how like his mother young Fred looked, and how pale he was. 'Pining, I reckon,' she thought to herself, 'pining for his Mam. It's been a long time.' Aloud, she said cheerfully, 'You'll have some milk before you go, Fred. And Alice, you'd best stop thinking about mice and circuses or you'll be having nightmares again. Your Dad will be going along to the post office in the morning and he'll be able to see what the notice says. Now drink up your milk, all of you. Your uncle will see you home, young Fred.'

[12]

Fred received his drink gratefully, but he did not at all want to be seen home by anybody. He was determined to have one more look into the snow house that night, by himself. He did not want even Alice to be with him. He looked up at

96

Auntie Patty over the rim of his mug. 'I can go back by myself,' he said. 'I'm old enough.'

Uncle John had come into the kitchen in time to hear what Fred said. Looking at the boy's earnest face, he chuckled at Auntie Patty, and gave Fred a light slap on the back of his jacket. 'Grown up, we are, are we?' he said. 'I reckon you're a big enough lad, right enough, young Fred. Off you go then, if you don't want my company. I'll sit by the fire and toast my toes.' His teasing grin won an answering smile from Fred, whose love for his uncle was so deep and strong that there could be no misunderstanding between them. He finished his milk and put on his coat. Auntie Patty tucked his scarf into his collar and dropped a good-night kiss on his head.

''Night, Fred,' said Alice. And, 'See you tomorrow,' Willie called across the kitchen. Auntie Patty stood for a few minutes in the open doorway, watching him trotting away across the Square, and Fred turned to wave before she closed the door. Then the night belonged to him. He was alone at last, and he trudged purposefully towards the snow house.

He stood beside it, listening, holding his breath. He stooped to peer in at the dark windows, and squatted in the carriage drive, pushing his nose against the door. He whispered, his mouth close to the tiny entrance, very softly. 'Is anybody there? It's me, Fred. Is there anybody ... anybody at all?'

Only the faint crackle of the snow as the night frost set upon it once more answered him. He strained his ears until he thought they would burst, but could hear nothing else. With a deep sigh he began to get to his feet, when suddenly he heard, from inside the snow house, a faint scratching sound. He stood absolutely still, not daring to breathe, and listened. The scratching came again, just inside the doorway,

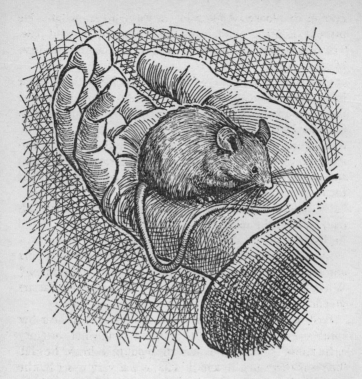

and as his heart jumped right up into his mouth he heard, unmistakably, a mouse's squeak. It was the smallest and highest of squeaks, and Fred knew, without any doubt at all, who it was.

'Singleton,' he cried, his whole body flooded with joy. 'Oh Singleton, you're still here. Come out to me, Singleton. I'll look after you till we find the others. Come out, won't you, please?'

Either the little mouse recognized Fred's voice, or he had learnt to understand at least some human language, or he was merely driven by desperate hunger. Fred could not tell, and he did not really care when he saw two small bright eyes in the doorway, gleaming in the faint snowlight. He put out his finger and felt the touch of a tiny trustful paw. The next instant the little mouse was crouched in the curve of his hand.

Cradling the mouse, Fred felt in his pocket with his other hand. One of the apples he had stowed away earlier in the day was still there. He bit off a small piece and offered it to Singleton who devoured it eagerly, sitting up on his haunches in Fred's hand and holding it daintily between his two front paws. Fred gazed at him lovingly, forgetting all about the capture of the other mice and the problem of their rescue in his delight.

He suddenly became aware of a small black shadow at his feet, and felt the touch of a soft furry body weaving round his legs.

'And what,' said Puss, in a voice halfway between a purr and a crow, 'is the meaning of this, I should like to know? What has become of my old friend Caradoc, and what are you doing with that child?'

Fred was immensely relieved to see her and to hear her speak again, and he started to pour out as much of the story as he knew. 'A man stole them all to put in a circus,' he said. 'Ben was there and he told us and he was very upset but he couldn't do anything – he's too little – and the circus is tomorrow on the Sally Lunn and we're going to get them back, Alice and Willie and me. I found Singleton here all by himself. The man must have missed him. We'll have to take him home, Puss, won't we?'

Puss did not reply directly. She spoke to Singleton in a language Fred could not follow, and the little mouse answered in a series of squeaks. Puss turned back to Fred.

'It seems,' she said, 'that before Caradoc was taken, he managed to push this child into a hole in the snow house, leaving him with instructions to come only to you or to me.' She licked the little mouse's head very gently. 'He seems intelligent, and he has been well taught. He can understand a great deal of what you say, though he is not yet able to speak your language. He may be very useful,' she added thoughtfully, 'but at the moment, as you say, we must take him home. And the easiest way is for me to take him.' She spoke again to Singleton, who shivered slightly but looked dutifully up at Puss; and Puss looked up at Fred, uttering a curious sound that was almost like a laugh.

'I am going to catch a mouse,' she said. She bent over the crouching Singleton, picked him up in her mouth, and danced away across the snow with his limp body hanging below her whiskers. Fred followed in wonder, and as they both reached the door of The Sundial Aunt Jen opened it and saw them coming.

'I thought you'd got lost, boy,' she said. 'I was just coming to look for you. Past your bedtime by a long way, and you've got to go to school in the morning. My goodness ...' she stared with distaste at Puss who leapt lightly in ahead of Fred with the little mouse in her mouth. 'A mouse, I do declare. Well, well –' with grudging approval. 'It's about time that cat earned its keep.' She shook her apron at Puss. 'Take it upstairs and eat it there. Nasty dirty things ...' and as Puss disappeared through the shop doorway she turned back to Fred. 'You'll have had your supper, I expect?' Fred nodded as he took off his coat and hung it on the hook. 'You'd better be getting to bed then. Say good night to your Dad.'

Fred's father had put down his book, taken his pipe out of his mouth, and was staring in open-mouthed astonishment at the sight of Puss with a mouse, and even more at young Fred's apparent disregard of her behaviour and of the mouse's plight. Fred went across to him and put his hand on his sleeve. He rubbed his nose against his father's cheek, and whispered close to his ear. 'It's all right, Dad. She won't hurt him.' Then in a louder voice, 'Good night, Dad.'

His father gave him a long look. Then he scratched Fred's head with the stem of his pipe, and said 'Good night, lad. I'll come up in a few minutes before you go to sleep.' His blue eyes looked again into Fred's and Fred looked down at his feet.

'Good night, Aunt Jen,' he mumbled, and went upstairs in a hurry.

In his cold bedroom Fred undressed as quickly as he could, fumbling with his buttons and laces. He climbed into bed, and curled himself gratefully round the warm brick in its flannel jacket that Aunt Jen had put in. In a few minutes he heard his father's footsteps on the stairs. When Dad came in, only Fred's eyes and the tip of his nose were visible above the bedclothes. His father sat down on the chair by the bed, stuck his empty pipe into his mouth, and looked down at his son.

'Well, young Fred?' he said.

'There's a circus on the Sally Lunn tomorrow,' began Fred hastily. 'It's a Mouse Circus, Dad. Alice and Willie are going. Can I go, Dad? We'd take Ben as well. After school, it is. Please, Dad?' His eyes looked warily at his father over the edge of the sheet.

'I dunno, young Fred.' Dad looked at him very thoughtfully, his pipe gripped between his teeth. 'It's a funny thing. I thought our mice were friends of yours. Now in comes Puss with a mouse she's caught and you don't turn a hair. Come to think of it, I've never known our Puss catch a mouse before. What's going on, lad?'

Fred began to stammer out half an explanation. 'It's all right. Puss won't hurt that mouse, Dad, really she won't. She only plays. Please Dad, can I go to the Mouse Circus?'

His father continued to look curiously at him. 'Your Aunt Jen,' he said at last, 'would say you had a fever. She might be right, at that. Mouse Circus? What kind of a thing is that? What would mice do in a circus?'

Fred's lip trembled. He dreaded to think what the mice would have to do, and little Ben's description of their capture, even related at second hand by Willie, made him fear that they might all be dead before they ever reached the Sally Lunn. Perhaps the man really intended to eat them for his supper. Tears of misery glistened in his eyes.

'Whey-ey, young Fred,' said Dad. He took his pipe out of his mouth and beat out a little tune with it on the top of Fred's head. 'No need to get upset. Alice and Willie are going, you say? I expect you'll go with them, then, whatever it is. You tell me all about it so I can tell Mam on Saturday.' He rubbed Fred's hair in a kind of inarticulate affection, not knowing what was troubling his son but anxious to cheer him up. 'There won't be so many more Saturdays for me to go to the hospital now,' he went on. 'Mam'll be home, and you can tell her all about your mice and your circuses and all. It's time you went to sleep, my lad, and stopped daydreaming. Aunt Jen will have my supper ready. 'Night, young Fred.' He got up and waved his pipe at Fred. 'Don't be late in the morning,' he said from the doorway with a grin, and went softly down the stairs.

Fred had been determined to stay awake, because he was sure Puss would come; but try as he would to keep his eyes open they grew heavier and heavier and he was asleep in a few minutes. He did not rouse when Aunt Jen came in to see him, nor when his father looked in on his way to bed. It was not until the early dawn light was glimmering through the window that he felt the touch of a soft padded paw on his cheek, and heard a vibrant purring in his ear. He woke with a start and saw Puss sitting on his counterpane with Singleton crouched by her side. He sat up, rubbing his eyes.

Puss began to speak at once, clearly and with great decision.

'Wake up, young Fred. The night is nearly over and there is a great deal to be done. What do you have in mind, you and your cousins, for the rescue of our captive friends?'

Fred struggled up with difficulty from the depths of sleep.
'We haven't anything in mind really,' he answered mournfully. 'We've just got to get them out somehow. We've got
to find where they are first, though.'

'I have done that already,' said Puss. 'They are all in the
circus cart. I could not get in and I dared not speak to them
for fear of rousing the dog, but I heard them squeaking
inside.'

'Oh Puss, Puss,' wailed Fred, now fully awake, 'whatever shall we do? How can we get to them?'

'There is only one thing to be done,' answered Puss firmly.
'You must go to the circus tomorrow, all of you. And you
must send this child in to find out what happens inside the
cart. Until you know that, you can't make any plans. Once
you know how the mice are kept you can plan their escape
before the circus moves on.'

'Singleton?' Fred cried in alarm. 'But we couldn't. He's
too little. We might lose him too, and he's the only one left.
We can't send Singleton.'

Puss looked gravely at him. 'Do not underestimate him,'
she said, 'and do not try to possess him. He belongs to his
own people and not to you, and you would do well to remember that. My young friend, with the best of intentions
you have put the rest of his tribe at risk. You have made
them your toys and your pets, and destroyed their wild and
frugal life. It will not do. They are a free people, and must
go their own ways.'

Young Fred, chastened and ashamed, looked at the little
mouse on the counterpane and pleaded desperately against
what seemed like a sacrifice. 'But Singleton is so small,' he
said, 'and he'll be all alone, going in there.'

'Singleton,' said Puss, 'is both intelligent and courageous.
I have talked to him about it and he is willing to go. He will
be very much afraid, of course; but there is no courage with-

out fear, and it is a good thing for his own protection, to be afraid. Once mice lose their fear they lose their chance of survival, as you have now learnt, I hope. You must send him in, because if you don't he will go by himself, in greater danger still. He comes of a line of princes, remember, and he is very proud.'

Fred looked down once more at the little mouse crouched at Puss's feet. Singleton did not look in the least proud or princely at that moment. He was shivering and trembling, and kept looking fearfully up at Puss as she talked. Fred swallowed his own tears, and finally managed to say, 'All right, Puss. We'll do as you say. I'll take him to the circus tomorrow. How will I take him, though?'

Puss looked down at Singleton and up at Fred. 'Ask him,' she said. 'He will tell you.'

Fred did not need to ask. The tiny mouse jumped off the bed and in a series of leaps and bounds landed on Fred's jacket which was hanging on the back of the chair. He climbed up the dangling sleeve and disappeared into the top pocket. Then his face popped out again, looking anxiously over the edge at Fred.

Young Fred suddenly laughed in relief and pleasure and affection, and Puss began to purr. 'He won't be able to tell me, Puss, but he can tell you and you can tell me and then we'll get all the others out, won't we? Alice will think of something, I know she will. She always does.' His eyes were beginning to close and he was getting sleepy again, so sleepy that everything began to swim away from him. The last thing he remembered was the face of Singleton peeping out of his pocket, and the sound of Puss purring in his ear.

'And don't forget,' he heard her murmuring as he fell asleep, 'I shall be there too.'

It had been a nightmare of a journey for the mice after they were snatched from the snow house and thrust into the canvas bag. The bag was pushed into the little black cart, and they were all bumped and joggled about as the man trundled along towards the Council Field. But worse was to come. Jem Leary, when he arrived at his destination, brought the cart to a standstill outside the wooden hut which he had hired for the show. It was a small but useful building standing at the far end of the Sally Lunn in the shelter of a semi-circle of scrubby thorn trees, and was known by the rather pretentious title of the Parish Hall. In the summer it served as a cricket pavilion, and at Christmas it was melodious with carols. In between times it was used for meetings, concerts and the school Prize Day, and hired out to visiting theatrical companies. There was a raised platform at one end on which stood an ancient piano with yellowed and sticky keys. Two paraffin stoves took the frost out of the air and steamed up the windows. There was also a spacious additional room which could be used as a kitchen, a cloakroom, a storeroom, a dressing room for performers, or a stable. 'Here we are, then, Bullseye,' grunted Jem Leary as he jerked the cart to a stop, 'and here we must bide.'

The first thing he did was to unhitch the donkeys who had been patiently trotting along behind the cart. Delighted at being released, they began to gambol and frolic, tumbling over each other in the snow, the dog barking at their heels. Jem Leary dragged a bundle of hay out of the cart, scattered a shovelful of oats on the ground, and left the donkeys feeding happily. Then, calling the dog, he lifted the back flap of the tarpaulin cover and pulled out his sleeping bag and a knapsack of provisions. He also took out a small cooking stove, went into the hall and with much grunting and groaning proceeded to make a meal for himself. He ate it at his leisure, feeding the whining dog with scraps from his plate, muttering under his breath about the cold and complaining at intervals about his feet. The mice were left in the cart all this time, huddled close together in the stifling canvas bag, shivering with fear. Caradoc and Almond tried to put some heart into them, though they themselves had little comfort to offer. The young Otleys became quite hysterical until Arthington managed to work his way through the crowd and put a stop to their wild squeaking by boxing their ears.

At last Jem Leary finished his meal. He dusted his hands together, saying, 'Well now, Bullseye boy, we'd better get

on with the job.' Accompanied by his snuffling dog, the
little man came out to the cart, extracted the bag of kicking,
squeaking mice, and gathered up a box of doll-sized furniture and costumes, an enormous pair of scissors, a spool of
fine wire and a ball of thread. He carried all this into the
hall, and perching himself on a chair by the stove, set to
work.

For so ugly and misshapen a man he had surprisingly
skilful hands. Picking up the mice one by one he delicately
tied loops of wire round their legs so that, though they remained captive, they could still run and jump in the small
space they were allowed. By an arrangement of sticks and
slip-knots, and clever manipulation of the wires with his
fingers, Jem Leary made string puppets of them all, and they
were forced to move when and where and how he wanted.

The younger ones jerked here and there as he practised, some dancing on their hind legs and some walking on their forefeet like diminutive acrobats. He made a number of the mice into trapeze artists, swinging dizzily to and fro. He tied others on to tiny chairs and by pulling the strings he made them clap their hands and cross their legs like an applauding audience. He attached a circle of mice to a maypole and made them dance round it, weaving a pattern with coloured ribbons while they ducked and bobbed. He tied a dozen of them together in lines of four, hung drums round their necks and attached matchsticks to their forepaws. When he pulled the fine wires they marched along together like a column of soldiers, beating their drums in unison. He mounted six mice on the backs of six others, and set them galloping round the ring like liberty horses.

He had a collection of little costumes in his box and proceeded to dress up the mice for the show. Some of them were rapidly transformed into clowns, with baggy trousers, conical hats and ruffs that fitted uncomfortably round their necks. On the head of each drummer he set a pillbox hat, and fitted scarlet coats on to their shoulders. He tied belts of tinsel and spangles round those on the trapezes, and put tiny plumes between the ears of the horses and their riders. It was all done at great speed and with remarkable dexterity, and as he finished dressing the mice he placed them in a row of cages which he had taken out of the cart.

There seemed no limit to his inventions. Within an hour he had arranged an act for all the mice except Almond, Arthington and Caradoc. Arthington, however, when he was finally picked up, turned suddenly on the man and gave his thumb a vicious bite. Jem Leary swore, stuck his thumb in his mouth and sucked it noisily, holding Arthington at arm's length in his other hand. Then he grinned.

'A fighter, eh?' he said. 'We'll make a better fighter of you, me boy. Trust Jem Leary.' With that he gripped

Arthington firmly while he tied a little pair of gloves on to the mouse's paws. He equipped Almond in the same way as a sparring partner, and staged a boxing match between them.

Then he looked at Caradoc. Something of the ancient chief's pride and dignity seemed to be conveyed to both Jem Leary and his dog. Bullseye crouched low on the ground and whimpered softly. The man hesitated for a moment, then shrugged his humpy shoulders and lifted Caradoc out of the bag.

'Well, milord,' he said, with a grating laugh. 'What about you, eh? You look an oldish buffer, you do. A bit grey about the muzzle. Top-hat and tails will do for you, I reckon. We'll have you for the Ringmaster.' His deft fingers wound the wire round Caradoc's legs and fitted on him a scarlet coat and an opera hat. 'How's that, Bullseye? He looks a swell. Pity he can't talk . . .' and he deposited Caradoc into the cage with the clowns. The black dog growled, and turned his head away.

'Right we are,' said Jem Leary, surveying his handiwork with satisfaction. 'All ready for the show. Supper time now, and then a bit of shut-eye, thank goodness.'

He carried the cages out of the hall and placed them carefully in the cart. Into each cage he put a tin of grain and broken bits of cheese and a little pot of water. He spread a large, rather dirty cotton cloth over the top of the cages, and lowering the flap at the back of the cart, tied it up securely. He called the donkeys and led them into the stable where he spread straw for their bedding. He tied old blankets round their shaggy bodies, fed them a handful of sugar lumps, and shut them in for the night. He returned to the hall with his dog, drew a small bottle from his coat pocket, screwed off the top, took two long gulps and blew out a weary breath. Then he unlaced his boots, and tucking his coat close around him, shuffled into his sleeping bag. He turned his coat collar up round his ears, muttering, 'Lie down, Bullseye.' Within a few minutes he was asleep, snoring loudly. The squeaking of the mice outside did not disturb him. He was used to it, and was not aware that there was a great deal of conversation going on. The dog knew quite well that the mice were talking to each other, but he was not able to understand what they were saying so he too slept, fitfully and with half an ear open, shivering with cold; until at last he crept into the sleeping bag with his master, and they lay close together, keeping each other warm.

Caradoc, though he felt very foolish dressed up in his top-hat and tails, retained his dignity, and made himself heard up and down the row of cages in the cart.

'My friends,' he said quietly, 'we have come to a pretty pass, I fear. We are imprisoned and in bonds, guarded by a dreadful gaoler. There is only one faint hope that I can offer. My grandson Singleton, as you have perhaps observed, has not been captured.'

There was an excited chattering from all sides. Most of the mice had been far too terrified to notice Singleton's absence. A few had been aware that he was missing, but fearing him to be dead, had not dared to speak of it. Only Arthington, Janus and the Cleveland-Tontines had seen him crouched in the farthest corner of the snow house behind Caradoc and Almond.

Caradoc continued, 'To the best of my knowledge he remains at liberty. He is very young, and he will be alone and no doubt very much alarmed. Before I was taken I gave him instructions to seek help from our ally Puss and from the boy Fred. Whether he will be able to do this I do not know, but I believe he will attempt it. Let us not, therefore, utterly despair.'

The mice rallied a little. They were by nature optimistic, and ready to clutch at any straw that was offered, and though every time they tried to move, their bonds reminded them of their dreadful plight, they had renewed their faith in Caradoc, and were bitterly ashamed of their recent behaviour. Also they could reach the cheese provided by Jem Leary, which was some small comfort. They were too exhausted by their experiences to do anything but nibble gratefully at their supper and hope for the best. Caradoc himself was unable to swallow anything; but he spoke gently to the tired company.

'Let us now rest, and hope. Who knows what tomorrow may bring?'

[14]

Alice sat on Benjamin's bed the next morning and gave him her orders before she went to school. 'Now don't you fret, Bennie, and no more crying, see. Willie and me are going to school, and we'll all go to the Sally Lunn after tea. We'll have a good time and we'll see the circus and Willie and you can ride the donkeys. We'll fetch those mice back soon and take them to the snow house. That's a secret, about the mice.' She laid her finger on Benjamin's lips. 'You musn't tell Mam or Dad or anybody, will you?'

Ben, only half awake, sat up in bed and stared goggle-eyed at his sister. He opened his mouth, shut it again, and then with a huge yawn and a sigh he settled down to finish his sleep. 'That's right,' he muttered as he buried his face in the pillow.

Alice looked at him and shook her head. Willie, who was standing shivering in his nightshirt, said, 'He doesn't talk much, anyway, only to himself. Nobody takes any notice.'

Auntie Patty's voice from down below sent them both scurrying. 'Willie – Alice –' she called. 'Your porridge is going cold.' They knew perfectly well that it was not. Their porridge would not be spooned out from the pan on the fire and put on to their plates until they were sitting at the table. It would be hot and steaming, too hot to eat, even when cream had been poured all over it; it was just their mother's usual warning that time was getting on. So they both gave their faces a hasty wash, put on their clothes and clattered downstairs, leaving Ben in bed.

'Mam,' said Willie, scraping his spoon round his porridge bowl, and already on his feet, 'can we take our tea to the circus?'

'For mercy's sake, you haven't finished your breakfast yet. And there's no need to eat it standing up. You can have your tea properly at the table before you go. There'll be plenty of time, surely. You can call for Fred after tea. Now wipe your mouth, Willie, and wash your hands. Here's your dinner ...' She packed two mutton pies and a bag of apples into the children's schoolbags. 'Come here, Alice, and I'll brush your hair. You haven't cleaned your boots ... and there's Fred here already.' The door had opened and young Fred's face was peeping round it. He looked pale and serious, and fidgeted from one foot to the other as he waited for his cousins.

'You're early, young Fred,' said Auntie Patty. 'Here, lad. Put this in your pocket for your dinner.' She tucked into the pocket of Fred's coat a little golden China orange, sweet-smelling and aromatic. Fred patted his pocket and smiled up into Auntie Patty's flushed and friendly face, as he stood watching her brushing Alice's dark hair. At last they were all ready, scarves and gloves wrapping them against the cold, clean handkerchiefs folded into the schoolbags that bumped up and down on their backs as they went slipping and sliding on their way to school.

As they crossed the Square they looked sadly at the snow house, now tenantless and deserted, and Fred told his cousins about the rescue of little Singleton and all that Puss had said the night before. 'Puss says they'll have to go somewhere else and look after themselves without us,' Fred said rather gloomily. 'She says we musn't keep them. I don't know where they could go to.'

Alice scuffed the snow impatiently with the toes of her boots, reluctant to lose her pets. 'They'll have to come back till we can find another place, though,' she said. But by this time the children had reached the school gates and the old iron bell that hung above its roof was calling them in its slow tolling voice, so they had to wait until dinner-time before they could talk any more.

There were two classes in the school, 'Big ones' and 'Little ones'. Willie and Alice were in the top class, and Fred, who was with the 'Little ones', did not see them again until midday. The classes were in fact in one large room, but they sat with their backs to each other, two tall cupboards and a long deal table dividing them. Between the two classes, against the wall, was a huge coke fire guarded by an enormous iron cage. It glowed like a furnace and gave out a tremendous heat. The children who sat nearest to the fire became so hot that their faces grew flushed and damp, and at half-hourly intervals everybody changed places so that the whole school warmed up and cooled off by turns. At midday all the children clustered round the fire to eat their lunches. Pies were warmed up round the edges of the fireguard. Slices of bread and dripping, impaled perilously on pen-holders or bits of wire, were extended towards the heat until the dripping ran off the bread and the slices grew crisp and dry. The children's faces became scarlet from the warmth, and they went thirstily to where there was water to drink, cold and sweet, from an iron cup attached by a chain to a tap at the end of the schoolroom.

An hour was allowed for dinner, and after they had eaten, the children were all sent outside to play. Fred and Alice and Willie retreated to the bottom of the school yard to talk. Willie, striding as usual up and down, said without any preamble, 'You'll bring him then, young Fred.' Fred was used to his cousin's habit of finishing his thoughts out loud, and knew he was referring to Singleton.

'I can put him in my pocket,' he replied, 'when I've had my tea. He won't mind.'

Alice was sitting on the wall, drumming her heels against it, and making plans. 'What we'll do,' she said; 'we'll go to the circus. Then, when it's finished, Willie can take Ben to the donkeys and me and Fred can go to the mice in the cart. Singleton can go in and tell the others and we'll wait till he comes back out and bring him home.'

Like all Alice's schemes, it sounded so simple. But – 'What about the dog,' said Willie. 'He'll be on the loose, won't he?'

'Bones,' replied Alice without hesitation. 'Dogs like bones. We'll get some.'

'Bones?' echoed Fred as the school bell called them in and they went back to the classroom. 'Bones, Alice? Where from?'

'Why, the bakehouse of course,' said Alice with a toss of her head. 'There's always bones for broth.'

The afternoon seemed interminable to Fred. His efforts at reading were so poor that his teacher asked him if he did not feel well, and when he said he did, he had to stand by the blackboard in front of the others while he 'thought about trying harder'. But Fred could only think about Singgleton and the awful prospect before him. At last the bell rang. The two classes stood up, put away their books and slates and the thin grey pieces of slate pencil that had been squeaking on fifty slates all day. The children turned about and faced each other. The teacher struck her desk with a tuning fork and stood it on its end on the table. A low humming sound issued from it, and the teacher imitated the note; 'M..M..M..me..me..me..' she intoned, and the school joined in. They sang a hymn, then prayed politely for the Lord's help in their weekend conduct at home. With heads bowed, they received a blessing which ended abruptly with the cheerful cry, 'Dismiss.' The children all tumbled out into the school yard, and Fred ran to catch up with Willie and Alice who were waiting for him at the gate.

Trudging home in the cold air, they had little to say. Willie kicked at the snow and kept his head down. Young Fred pushed his hands deep into his pockets and thought about the little mouse who would soon be stowed away there. Even Alice's jaunty confidence seemed to have evaporated. Fred left the others at the corner and went on alone to The Sundial, and nobody said a word.

[15]

In the kitchen Aunt Jen was making scones for tea, and Puss, to Fred's surprise, was sitting on the rug by the fire washing her paws. As Fred came in she looked up and gave a little crow of welcome.

'That cat,' said Aunt Jen, 'has been there all afternoon, idling about instead of doing her job in the cellar catching mice. Too well fed.'

'She did catch one though, didn't she Aunt Jen?' Fred said with an unusual glint of mischief in his eyes as he stroked Puss's shining fur.

'H'm. There's plenty more where that came from. Nasty dirty things ...' Aunt Jen rubbed the end of her nose in fastidious disapproval and popped the scones into the oven. 'You'd better be washing your hands, boy. These won't be ten minutes. Hang your coat up and take your boots off, and run and tell your father not to be long. You're off out again tonight, he says. Why you want to go out in the dark I don't know ... catch another cold most likely ... in bed again and what will your Mam say ...' she rambled on in a grumbling soliloquy. Young Fred washed his hands at the kitchen sink and went through to the shop to call his father.

All through tea Fred watched the clock. The hands hardly seemed to move at all, and as he chewed his scones he wished he could jump half an hour so that the time would go faster. Willie and Alice were calling for him at six; but tea was over by five and there was a long time to wait. He helped Aunt Jen with the dishes, and ten more minutes went by. Dad fished some money out of his pocket and gave it to him, saying, 'Here, young Fred. That's enough for the donkeys and some sweets if you can find any.' He suddenly looked at Puss, and said, 'Hadn't you better take her upstairs before you go?'

Puss rose from the rug, stretched her legs, and went straight to Fred. He lifted her up so that she could put her paws round his neck and sit in the crook of his arm, and climbed the catsteps, carrying her up to the loft. Once at the top of the ladder Puss leapt lightly from Fred's arms and crossed the floor towards the far corner of the room, ignoring the kittens who had embarked on a joyful chorus of welcome.

It was then that Fred witnessed a remarkable sight. In the remote shadows of the loft crouched Singleton, his ears erect with fear, his whiskers stiff and his whole body taut. Puss stooped over him and gathered him up. Holding the frightened mouse in the curve of her paw, she nestled him in the soft fur under her chin, her mouth close to his head. For a few minutes Fred thought she was merely breathing in his ear, as she often did with the kittens to comfort them; but as he watched he realized that she was talking to him in a low murmur, and though Fred did not understand the language she used, he knew by the sound of her voice what was happening. She was instructing Singleton, encouraging him, reassuring him, consoling him. Fred watched and listened, hardly daring to breathe, until at last Puss raised her head. Then he stretched out his hand. Puss picked up the small mouse in her mouth and placed him in Fred's out-stretched palm. Singleton, with a last resigned shiver, curled himself into a ball in Fred's hand. Fred put him very carefully into his pocket, and looked solemnly at Puss.

'He knows, does he?' he asked. But Puss, only purring in response, went over to the kittens and began to wash them, one by one.

Fred stood irresolute for a few minutes, his mind filled with anxiety and his heart heavy with responsibility. The fate of a whole tribe of mice seemed to depend on Singleton, his cousins and himself, and he was almost afraid to go. He fingered the pocket where the mouse lay hidden, and at last he turned and climbed down the ladder and down the cat-steps to the kitchen.

'You'd better hurry up, young Fred,' said his father. 'There's Willie and Alice at the door now, coming for you.' And there they were, with Benjamin swathed in his scarf, impatient to be gone. Aunt Jen helped Fred into his coat, wrapped his scarf round his neck and pulled his cap on to his head, and they were all away, running from the lamplit kitchen into the moonlit Square.

Slipping and sliding over the frozen ground, they were too breathless to talk much. Alice was clutching a lumpy parcel under one arm. 'What is it – what's that, Alice?' gasped Fred, poking it with an inquisitive finger as they ran along.

'Marrow bones,' replied Alice, whispering although there was nobody within earshot. 'Bones for the dog, like I said.'

The Parish Hall was just over a mile beyond the Square, at the far end of the Sally Lunn. When the children reached the edge of the field they could see, over the curving slope, the dim glow of the oil lamps shining out through the windows, and the bright bobbing lights of a host of storm lanterns pricking the darkness outside. 'Lots of folks,' said Willie, slowing his pace to a walk. 'Let's go round the back and look for the cart.'

He led the way across the field and the others followed, threading their way among the crowds of children who were all moving towards the front entrance of the hall, chattering at the tops of their voices, eager to get inside. The door was still closed, and there was a large notice nailed on to it:

MOUSE CIRCUS

THIS WAY IN.

They went stealthily round the side of the wooden hut and Willie peeped round the next corner.

'It's here,' he muttered under his breath, and creeping close behind him Fred and Alice could see the little cart propped up on its shafts under the thorn trees. Ben uttered a sharp cry of fear as the sight of it brought back the awful memory of the previous afternoon's horror; and, indeed, it looked very dark and sinister in the moonlight, with its black cover tightly fastened down and the huge white-painted letters clearly visible on its side. The two donkeys were tethered to one of the shafts, their shaggy coats drenched in moonshine, and both their noses buried in a sack of hay that hung up on a nail at the front of the cart. The dog was nowhere to be seen.

'Where can he be?' whispered Fred. 'He can't be in that cart. Perhaps he's tied up somewhere.'

'He'll be loose, more likely,' said Willie. 'You stay here a minute. I'll go round the other side and see.' He stole forward, crept round the back of the cart and disappeared from view. Alice and Fred, with Benjamin pressed between them, waited, holding their breath.

The next moment the back door of the hall opened, letting out a shaft of yellow lamplight; letting out also Jem Leary, followed by his dog, just as Willie was emerging from the darkness behind the cart. The dog began to bark wildly and hurled itself in Willie's direction. Alice gave a little shriek and started forward, letting go of Ben's hand. Fred was too frightened to move at all and stood staring in terror at the little man in the battered top-hat who rolled his eyes at each of them in turn.

'Now then, young lady and young gentlemen,' Jem Leary said in his husky voice, 'what might you be doing round here, eh? Bullseye, come back here. It's only a boy. We don't want no trouble.' The dog drew back, and crouched, snapping and growling, at its master's feet, its eyes roving suspiciously from Willie to the others. 'You've no business round here,' the man went on. 'The way in's round the front. You go round to the front and wait your turn.'

Willie took a step forward, but stopped hurriedly as the

dog drew itself together and bristled. 'We ... we wanted to see your donkeys,' he stammered. 'We thought you had donkey rides.'

'After the show, young gentleman, after the show. Three-pence a go. Now you take yourselves off, if you please. You've no business round the back here. Why ... bless my life and soul ...' he suddenly caught sight of Benjamin, and the grin that spread over his face was if anything more hideous than his scowl. 'Why, there's our young gentleman who did us a good turn, Bullseye.' He squinted at Ben and uttered his harsh laugh. 'Never forget a friend. You shall go in for free, so you shall.' He shambled over to the children and pressed a sixpenny piece into Ben's hand. 'Always trust Jem Leary,' he said with a leer. 'You'll tell your Mammy and your Daddy that you had a free seat, won't you? Now off to the front door with you and get your tickets. Nearly time to start ...' He shooed them away, flapping his hands at them; then turned and went inside again by the back door, leaving the black dog loose outside.

Fred's heart was thumping against his ribs and his hand closed protectively round the little mouse in his pocket as he looked back at the black cart. Alice clutched the parcel of bones to her chest with both hands. Benjamin had come out into the open and was standing with his feet planted squarely on the frozen ground, gazing up into the branches of the scrubby thorn trees beneath which the circus cart rested. Willie had begun to retreat towards the others, keeping a wary eye on the dog.

'Come on,' he muttered, 'Let's go. Come on, Ben.'

Benjamin continued to stare up into the trees. 'There's a house up there,' he announced in a clear high voice. 'Like your sewing basket, Alice. But it's got a roof on.'

'Come on,' repeated Willie urgently; and then suddenly, his eyes following Ben's gaze, he stopped short. 'It's a nest,' he murmured softly to himself. 'A magpie's nest, big and empty. I reckon they could all get in there.' With a jump of excitement, he clapped his little brother on the shoulder. 'You're a clever lad, our Ben, that you are, though you don't know it. That's it, Fred. There's a mouse house if ever there was one. Now come on. Let's go or we'll miss the circus.' He marched off, pushing Ben ahead of him, round the side of the Parish Hall towards the front entrance and the dancing lights and the chatter of children pushing their way in. Alice and Fred followed him closely, and they were soon in the middle of the noisy jostling crowd.

It was not long before they had pushed their way inside with all the others. The circus man, whom they had last seen disappearing through the back door, was now at the front, taking the money and dropping it into a blue canvas bag tied on to his rope belt. Ben gave him his sixpence back, and Jem Leary patted him on the head with his grimy horny hand. 'That's right, young gentleman,' he croaked at him. 'Enjoy yourself and tell your Mammy to let you come again tomorrow, eh? It's a lovely show ... never seen anything like it. Trust Jem Leary.'

Benjamin shrank away from his touch, but Willie said cheerfully, 'Oh yes, we'll be coming again tomorrow. Look out for us.' Jem Leary looked after them with sudden suspicion.

'You'll have to pay your way, young gentleman. No more free tickets, mind.'

'Come on,' said Willie, ignoring him and pressing forward with the other children, 'let's get near the front.'

It was easier said than done. Inside the Hall a faint blue haze hung on the air, and the smell of the paraffin stoves was thick and warm. Everybody surged towards the far end, where the piano was at one side of the platform, and a tall box like a Punch and Judy show stood in the middle. It had sides made of red and white striped canvas, and faded green velvet curtains were drawn across the front. There were a few mats for the audience to sit on, one or two folding benches, and a dozen or more canvas chairs in rows at the back. A few parents and other adults occupied the chairs and benches, while all the children clustered on to the mats or close behind, kneeling up or sitting on their heels, craning their necks in order to see, and breathing heavily into each other's ears. Willie managed to push Alice and Ben on to a mat on the third row, and he and Fred stood up at the side, shuffling their feet with impatience. While they waited Willie had time to whisper into Fred's ear.

'Listen, Fred.' Willie's voice was quiet but authoritative. 'Ben saw that magpie's nest, didn't he? I reckon there'd be room for all the mice in there for a while. It'd be a bit of a squash but they'd manage. We'll never get them all the way back to the snow house on Saturday night. It's too far. You'll have to tell your Singleton to give them the message. Ben and me will go for the donkey rides after, and you and Alice can send Singleton in to tell the others. We'll come back tomorrow and get them into the magpie's nest after the show.'

Fred was full of misgivings and uncertainty. 'Won't the man be looking for them though?' he said doubtfully. 'How can we get them in there without him seeing?'

'It'll be Saturday night, won't it,' hissed Willie, 'and I reckon he'll be going on somewhere else after the show. He'll likely put all the mice in the cart ready to move off. There's choir in the Parish Hall at nine o'clock so he'll have to get out. Oh look, he's starting.'

Fred looked at Willie in grateful admiration. He would never himself have remembered the choir-practice, and even if he had he would not have put two and two together and realized that the circus man would have to be gone by then. But Willie's lively mind was always a jump ahead. Maybe it was because he talked so much and never sat still, thought Fred, that he was so quick to see chances; and he gave the little mouse in his pocket an encouraging pat. Willie tapped him on the arm. 'Look,' he repeated softly, and Fred stared up at the platform.

Jem Leary had appeared in front to the accompaniment of cheers and whistles. He grinned at the audience, waving his arms. 'Now, young ladies and young gentlemen, silence if you please. Must have silence. Noise makes my actors nervous.' He leered round at the children's upturned faces, and a hush fell upon the company. Jem Leary shuffled his feet. 'Anybody play the piano?' he asked hopefully. 'My actors like a bit of music.' A hesitant murmur went round and a few children giggled. Finally a stout rosy-faced lady got to her feet, left her children to look after themselves, and stumped over to the piano. She drew off her gloves, rubbed her hands, opened the piano lid and sat down on the stool.

'What do you want me to play?' she asked, looking nervously over the piano at the little circus man.

Jem Leary waved his hands airily. 'Don't matter, ma'am,' he said. 'Anything that takes your fancy as long as it's cheerful. Nice to have a bit of a tune. Right, we're off. Young ladies and young gentlemen, sit up and wait for it now. The one and only Mouse Circus. Never seen anything like it. Trust Jem Leary.' And with a final flourish of his hands he vanished behind the little box of a stage. There was a scuffling and squeaking behind the velvet curtains; the lady at the piano struck up a rousing march; the audience, open-mouthed with anticipation, gazed up at the stage; and with a series of shaky jerks the curtains were drawn back to reveal a miniature circus ring complete with tiny ladders, swinging trapezes, buckets and brooms and sawdust, and a semi-circle of little chairs on which were perched half a dozen small mice dressed in coats and hats and white silk scarves, all clapping their front paws together in inaudible applause. The children watching gasped in admiration and joined in the applause themselves, clapping loudly.

Into the centre of the stage came Caradoc, walking on his hind legs, resplendent in his top-hat and scarlet coat. Fine, almost invisible strings controlled every movement he made. He marched up and down cracking his tiny whip and bowing to the audience, then moved backwards off the stage out of the ring while Jem Leary's grating voice announced above the thumping of the piano, 'Make way for the Dare-Devils ... finest acrobats in the world.'

Fred felt sick. The bright round eyes of the performing mice were starting out of their heads with terror. Caradoc's whiskers had never stopped trembling though his head had been held proudly up, and the spectacle of the ancient noble chief, tied hand and foot and forced to dance like a puppet on a string in front of his own people made Fred's hair prickle on his scalp. The little group of trapeze artists swung perilously to and fro in the air, tied to the ropes that hung from the top of the stage. One act followed another; the clowns tumbled over and over, throwing paste and water at each other and falling flat on their faces, making the audience roar with laughter. The liberty horses galloped round and round the ring, their riders clinging to their backs or balancing precariously while the horses reared up and danced on their hind legs. A troupe of jugglers balanced plates on their noses and threw balls into the air, catching them on their tails. In between the acts Caradoc was brought on again to cavort about the ring cracking his whip, while all the time the little mice on the ringside seats were made to clap and jump excitedly up and down. Willie stood unusually still, a dark scowl on his face. Alice was biting her lip as she knelt on the mat, clutching Ben's hand and holding on tight to her parcel of bones. Ben himself sat cross-legged, gazing in solemn wonder at the performance, unable to understand how these dressed-up mice could do such clever things. Fred, wondering if the nightmare would ever come to an end, kept his hand closely curled around Singleton, who crouched invisible in his pocket.

For nearly an hour the performance went on. The audience was ecstatic with delight, laughing and clapping and crowding closer and closer to the stage. The stout lady played on valiantly but was beginning to run out of music. She had exhausted her repertory of national songs and had started all over again on the march she had played at the beginning when Jem Leary's harsh voice announced loudly, 'Last turn now, young ladies and young gentlemen. Watch it now; the Greatest Fight On Earth. Zamba and Zambetti ... the two unbeatables.'

All this time Fred had been anxiously waiting to see what had happened to Almond, who had not yet appeared. As one turn followed another and there was still no sign of him, Fred was beset by fears that he might have been killed by the circus man, or devoured by the dog, or come to some other terrible end. Then at last he was there, his paws encased in tiny boxing gloves, dancing stiffly in the ring with Arthington as his partner. Round and round each other they went, ducking and feinting and landing light blows on each other's heads. As Fred watched Almond jumping painfully about on his injured leg it was all he could do to hold back his tears. He shut his eyes and waited miserably for the wretched performance to end; and at last it did. Arthington lay panting, and apparently defeated, while Almond shook his gloved paws above his head in triumph. The green velvet curtains were drawn uncertainly together across the scene. The stout lady played a final chord and leaned back in obvious relief, while the audience clapped and shouted and stamped and whistled as Jem Leary's stumpy figure appeared in front once more.

'Thank you kindly, ma'am. Thank you, young ladies and young gentlemen. That's the end of my show. Now give me five minutes, if you please, and get your money ready. I'll just put my friends to bed and any young lady or young gentleman with threepence to spare can have a ride on my donkeys. Up and down the field for threepence, that's a bargain. Rides in the moonlight. Trust Jem Leary.' He flapped his hands at the children and hustled them all towards the front entrance. They began to jostle their way out to the field, while the little circus man went back to the platform behind his Punch and Judy box. Willie and Fred had pushed through to the front of the crowd and were outside for some minutes before Alice had managed to struggle through with Ben.

'Get round to the side, Fred, quick, out of the light,' muttered Willie in Fred's ear. 'Alice'll come and find you. I'll take Ben.' Fred stumbled hastily away round the corner of the hut, not daring to go too near the back, and hid himself in the shadows to wait for Alice. He squatted down by the wall, and taking the little mouse out of his pocket he cradled him lovingly in both his hands, speaking in an urgent whisper.

'Tell Caradoc. Tell him we're coming. Tell him we'll come tomorrow and get them all away. Tell him not to be afraid. Tell him we've found a place for you all to hide. Tell him ... tell him ... oh Singleton, do you understand what I say? Alice and me will wait for you. We won't leave you, Singleton.' His mind was confused and the message was muddled, but it was the best he could do. He could hardly make out the mouse's shape in the darkness, but Singleton's body was taut in his hands and he seemed to be listening intently. Fred suddenly felt a touch on his sleeve and jumped in alarm.

'It's me,' said Alice's voice. 'He's coming to the front with the donkeys, so we can get round the back. I'll go first and see if the dog's there. You keep behind me. Put your hand in my pocket, Fred. There's my scissors in there. You can cut a little slit in the cart cover for that mouse to go in. We can cut it a bit bigger tomorrow for them all to come out. We'll have to cut those strings as well, I reckon. I wonder how we'll manage that. Never mind, we'll wait and see.'

They crept forward along the side of the Parish Hall until they could see the shape of the little black cart under the thorn trees. Fred seized Alice's coat. 'The dog's there,' he gasped. 'On the back step.'

The thin black dog sat shivering against the door, longing for his supper. He growled softly as they appeared, lifting the hair on the back of his neck in warning. Alice took a deep breath, unwrapped her parcel and stepped quietly towards the dog, holding out a handful of meaty bones. 'Here boy,' she said softly. 'Good boy, then. Here you are.' She dropped the juiciest bone at his feet. He lowered his head and sniffed it, then looked up at Alice, his eyes glistening with hunger and suspicion. The next moment he was ravenously chewing and tearing at the bone, holding it down with his front paws and crunching it with his teeth; and for the first time his tail began to wag, very slowly.

'Go on, Fred,' whispered Alice as she stepped closer to the dog. 'Good boy,' she said soothingly. 'There's a good boy.' The dog looked balefully at her, but he went on eating his bone and his tail continued to wag. Alice dropped another bone in front of him. He stopped, sniffed at it, and went on chewing. By now his matted tail was waving wildly in rapture, and Fred crept quietly away to the back of the cart. He stooped behind the wheels, and with the points of Alice's scissors he poked a hole through the bottom of the tarpaulin cover. Then he pushed Singleton in through the hole, and stood with his eyes glued to it waiting to see what would happen.

16

Inside the black cart Caradoc and his tribe were lying exhausted. The acrobatics they had been forced into had made them ache all over, the puppet strings had dragged at their legs and necks, and their small hearts were throbbing with fright. Jem Leary had been practising with them most of the day, preparing for the show. The mice had had very little rest and only a meagre supply of food. In addition they had discovered that there were other mice in the cart, prisoners like themselves, but prisoners who had been there, they said, for many days. When Caradoc and Almond succeeded in talking to them it was obvious that the other mice were not a tribe but a collection of individuals and families who had been captured at different times by Jem Leary and his dog.

'They don't last long,' Jem Leary had said; and indeed most of these mice did not look as though they would survive much longer. Their fur was thin and bedraggled and their tails hung limply down. They had a generally decrepit appearance, and had quite lost heart. Caradoc and Almond spoke to them of the possibility of rescue, but could not persuade them that there was any hope of escape. It was depressing company, and the younger mice in Caradoc's tribe were becoming very discouraged.

'Even if anybody does come to help us,' muttered Arthington, as he listened to the hopeless conversation, 'we'll never get this lot out. Might as well give up.' Caradoc looked at him gravely.

'It has never been our custom,' he said with some severity, 'to leave any members of our race in danger. If and when the time comes, it behoves us all to travel together.' Arthington was silenced but unconvinced.

Almond sighed. His damaged leg was aching dreadfully. He had been thinking all day about poor little Singleton, left alone and unprotected in the snow house. Hour after hour had gone by and there had been no sign of him, nor of Puss nor the boy Fred; and although he did his best to keep up the spirits of the others his own were at a very low ebb. He rested his chin wearily and uncomfortably on his front paws which were still encased in boxing gloves, and closed his eyes.

At that very instant he heard, from the back of the cart, an inquiring squeak.

*

Fred waited nearly half an hour at the back of the Parish Hall, watching for Singleton's return with his eyes riveted to the little hole in the cart cover. Alice joined him after a few minutes and they stood together, shivering and whispering. The dog lay peacefully on the doorstep chewing the last of the bones, its animosity dispelled. They could hear in the distance the jubilant shouts of the other children enjoying their donkey rides, while the moon was sliding away behind the thorn trees. It was getting late. Alice said, 'We'll have to go home in a minute. Can't you get him, Fred?' Fred stooped down and put his mouth to the hole in the canvas.

'Singleton,' he called desperately, 'Singleton. Come back ... come back quick.'

There was a scutter and a squeak from inside and the next moment the hole was full of mouse. Singleton pushed his way out and leapt into Fred's outstretched hands. Alice skipped up and down in excitement. 'Did you tell them?' she whispered. 'Are they all right? Did you find them?

What did they say?' She bent her face close to the little mouse, but Singleton only blinked in alarm, staring back at her with his bright round eyes. Fred closed his hand protectively round the little creature.

'He can't talk,' he said. 'I think he knows what we say but he can't say anything back ... only in mouse talk. Puss knows what he says, though.' Singleton pushed his sharp nose through Fred's fingers and began to utter little squeaks.

'Listen,' said Alice. 'Listen. He's trying to tell us something, I know he is.' She stooped once more to the tiny mouse, and a strand of her warm dark hair fell over his face. He lifted his chin, shook off the hair that tickled his nose, sneezed, and uttered a single word. 'Caradoc.'

Fred, with a cry of delight, put his other hand over Singleton and squeezed him with such excited affection that the little mouse almost had the breath knocked out of him. He choked, and crouched a little lower in Fred's hand.

Suddenly there was a great noise of shouting and laughing

and the sharp crunch of footsteps on the frozen snow. Fred pushed Singleton into his pocket just in time, and turned to see Willie and Ben who had come racing round the corner of the Hall with a crowd of other children, following Jem Leary who was leading his donkeys to bed.

'Now, young ladies and young gentlemen.' The little man's voice was hoarser than ever after all the talking he had done. 'Time you were all in bed. Time for my donkeys to go to sleep. Two thirty tomorrow you can see another show. You tell your mammies and your daddies and they'll bring you along. Go home now. That's enough for tonight.' The donkeys tripped cheerfully towards their stabling, hopeful of hay for supper, and nuzzled playfully at each other in the fading moonlight. The over-excited children gradually melted away and the bobbing storm lanterns began to disappear like will o' the wisps across the snowy field. 'All right, Fred?' said Willie. Fred nodded, and they all turned away, leaving the circus man and the little black cart and the quiet dog. Alice took hold of Ben's hand and set out for home, followed by the two boys. Ben turned his head and waved vaguely in the direction of the thorn trees.

'There's your cat, Fred,' he said.

Ben always saw what nobody else had noticed. Fred stopped short and stared through the darkness at where the little boy had pointed. A black shape, blacker than the branches, detached itself and slid down a tree-trunk, melting into the shadows. Fred took a deep breath. There indeed was Puss; and there, no doubt, she had been all the time, unseen by anybody.

She disappeared into the darkness and went home a different way.

17

The Sundial was dark and full of sleep. The faint sound of snoring could be heard coming from Dad's bedroom, and the occasional creak of the mattress as Aunt Jen turned restlessly in the night. Singleton was tucked safely away in the loft in a nest of sugar bags, and the kittens in their basket slept peacefully in each other's arms. Puss sat up on the end of Fred's bed, her eyes gleaming in the dark, while Fred recounted all that had happened that evening. He described the circus and the fancy costumes in which the mice were dressed. He told Puss about Alice's conquest of the black dog and about Willie's idea that the magpie's nest might be a temporary refuge for the mice when, and if, they were released from the cart; and about how he himself had managed to smuggle Singleton through the hole in the cover, and about the donkeys. Puss listened attentively, and translated for Fred's benefit all that Singleton had reported about his visit to the mice in the cart.

'From what I hear,' she said, 'the rescue you are planning will not be easy. All our friends are not only in cages but are bound in some way.' Fred tried to explain. 'There's wire tied round their legs and little sticks the man holds. The mice are all tied up to these to make them dance. It's dreadful.' He shuddered at the recollection of Almond pirouetting about the ring with his poor stiff leg dragging. 'But I thought he might undo them when he puts them inside.'

'It seems not,' said Puss grimly. 'The child tells me that they are all securely bound. It would be impossible for them to bite through all the bonds in time. Singleton was not able to get inside the cages, though he tried his best. He did, however, tell Caradoc that an attempt would be made to free them all before they are taken away from here, so everybody will be prepared.'

Fred hugged his knees. 'Whatever can we do, Puss? The cart's all locked up.'

'There you are wrong,' said Puss. 'It is fastened but not locked. I was able to look at it closely and I found it tied down with ropes. It can be untied. Teeth and claws can't do it, but fingers can.' She looked at Fred. 'You must open that cart.'

Fred looked back at Puss, fearful and bewildered. She went on before he could speak. 'Your cousin Alice has succeeded in winning the confidence of the dog. That, you know, was the cleverest thing she could have done and I must say I would never have thought of it.' She gave a little purr of approval. 'If she can keep his attention while the man has his donkeys out on the field, and you work very quickly, there may just be time for you to open the cart and go inside. Take the scissors, snip the wires and open the cages to let the prisoners out. It is up to them to make their own escape. Before the man comes back you must be sure that the cart is refastened so that he suspects nothing. There is still the hole in the back, remember, if everybody is not out in time.'

'Oh Puss,' said Fred, filled with misgivings, 'suppose I can't get the ropes off in time? Suppose the man sees me? Suppose that dog catches them? Suppose ...' but Puss stood up and suddenly seemed to grow to twice her size, speaking with as much authority as Caradoc.

'We shall not suppose anything at all,' she said. 'There are risks that must be taken and no good will come of supposing. In addition there are two other things to remember. Caradoc has got to be told of this plan, and of the magpie's nest he can lead his tribe to. There is only one person who can do this. Singleton must be taken to the circus and put into the cart before the performance begins. He is very

133

small and can hide without difficulty. And I myself will take him there. He can find his own way in. We shall start from the nest itself so that he can lead the way back to it. Also I will give him all the necessary instructions for Caradoc. There is one more thing. Apparently there are other mice in the cart, strangers to the tribe, and Caradoc insists that they are not left behind. As you may have noticed, once Caradoc has made up his mind, his word is law. But this is where I can be of no help at all. These mice do not know me, and if they should see me they are likely to panic and put everybody at risk. They are sure to regard me as their most terrible enemy. So I must not be seen. But, of course, I shall not be far away.'

Fred gazed at Puss in admiration after this long speech. 'You've thought of everything,' he said in wonder. 'But surely, Puss, Caradoc can tell the others that you are their friend?'

'They wouldn't believe it,' said Puss, 'and for their own future safety it is better that they shouldn't.' She sat down again and began to wash her paws. Knowing full well that this was a signal for her imminent departure, Fred began to talk fast.

'What are you going to tell Singleton?' he said. 'What will he say to Caradoc?'

Puss, her voice already beginning to lose its human tone, said briefly, 'I shall speak to him in his own language.' She yawned, stretched her legs, gathered herself up and with her usual grace leapt noiselessly off the bed. As she reached the doorway Fred made one last effort to keep her.

'Puss, Puss,' he called after her. 'How did you find out about the rope on the cart? I never saw you there.'

With a curious sound, halfway between a chuckle and a purr, Puss replied, 'You weren't intended to, young Fred.' And the next moment she was gone.

For a long time that night Fred lay awake. The thoughts

of what he had to do the next day went round and round in his head. He wished it could be tomorrow at once, and at the same time he was afraid of tomorrow's coming in case things went wrong. He went over in his mind all that Puss had said so that he could tell Alice and Willie, and all the while he was thinking about Caradoc and his friends in the chilly darkness of the circus cart, dressed in their gaudy finery and imprisoned in fine threads like flies in a spider's web. Tomorrow, too, things were happening in the real world. It was visiting day at the hospital and his father would be leaving early.

'It won't be much longer now, young Fred,' he had said when he came to say good night to his son. 'Not long now before your Mam comes home and I won't be spending my Saturdays on the train any more.'

'And then, and then,' thought Fred, 'the mice can all come home and they won't need to be frightened any longer. If we can only keep them safe till then.' He tossed and turned, and when at last he went to sleep he had strange dreams about the mice in the bird's nest, all dressed in clowns' hats with wings on their shoulders. When he woke it seemed colder than ever. Aunt Jen was calling from the kitchen, and he scuffled into his clothes and came downstairs, rubbing his eyes.

'You look half asleep,' said Aunt Jen as she spooned out his porridge, 'and as pale and pasty as a pudding. Does you no good going out at night this weather ... much better off indoors ... see the doctor again next week ... get you a bottle of Parrish's food. I suppose you'll be off to that circus again. Good thing it's in the daylight. You'll come straight home and be here for when your Dad comes back, mind. Don't know what you want to go gawping at mice for ... nasty dirty things ...' she swallowed her own tea as she talked, in hasty gulps as if it might escape from the cup unless she drank it quickly.

Dad grinned at Fred and got up from the table, pushing his plate away. 'Well, time I was off. Be a good lad, young Fred. I'll be home about six, I daresay.' The icy air swept into the kitchen when he opened the door. He cocked his head at the sky and pulled his hat down over his ears. 'There's a change in the weather on the way, I reckon. It's a raw morning.' Cold as he was, Fred stood in the open doorway and watched his father along the street, and waited until he turned at the corner to wave his hand.

'For goodness' sake, boy,' Aunt Jen complained, 'come inside and shut the door before we all perish;' and with a last look down the empty street Fred turned gratefully back to the kitchen fire.

The children had arranged that Fred should go to the bakehouse for dinner, but Aunt Jen kept him busy all morning doing various jobs. He had to tidy his toy cupboard, and dust the shop counters while she swept every vestige of oatmeal and sugar from the floor. 'It's no wonder we have mice all over the place,' she said severely, 'all these bits about. Might as well ask them to breakfast.' Fred was suddenly transported at the thought of a party of mice eating their porridge under Aunt Jen's supervision, and he gave a nervous little giggle. Aunt Jen frowned at him over her spectacles.

'It's no laughing matter, young Fred. But it's no good talking to your father. He's as soft as you are. Now take that duster upstairs and do your bedroom and don't forget the chair-legs.'

It was nearly midday before Fred could get away. He had not seen Puss all morning. There was no sign of her, nor of Singleton, when he had stolen quietly up to the loft. Only the kittens were there, scrambling in and out of the basket and boxing each others' ears as they tumbled about in friendly enmity. He wondered if the little mouse were already in the circus cart, and trembled for his safety. He thought about Puss, concealed somewhere in the cold, keeping faithful watch close by, and felt as though he would burst with impatience before the afternoon came. At last he was set free, bundled into his coat and scarf and given a hot brown lozenge to suck 'against the cold', and he slipped out into the Square. The lozenge burnt his tongue and he managed to spit it out as soon as he was out of sight. As he crossed the Square by the snow house it looked quite grey. The brightness had gone from the air; the sky was heavy and dull, and the snow had lost its sparkle. Fred trudged rather dispiritedly towards the bakehouse.

Willie was waiting for him in the bakehouse kitchen and began talking cheerfully before Fred had got inside the door. 'I thought you were never coming,' he said, twirling about on his heels and toes like a spinning top. 'What kept you then? Did you get lost or something? What a long time you've been. My, you do smell funny, Fred. Whatever have you been eating?' He sniffed distastefully, screwing up his nose. 'Aunt Jen gave me a hot lozenge,' said Fred, 'but I spat it out. It was horrible. Where's Alice?'

'Squills,' said Willie with another sniff. 'Fit to blow your head off. I don't know. She said she'd be back in a minute but she's been gone ages. There's only me and Ben.'

As far as Fred could see there was only Willie, but periodic rustlings and bumps under the table indicated where Ben was. Fred recounted all that Puss had told him and Willie listened attentively, his hands deep in his pockets. Finally, nodding his head, he said, 'So they'll all follow-my-leader up the tree. Can they climb, Fred? It's high, that nest.'

'I suppose so,' said Fred dubiously. 'I hope so. Puss says it's up to them, once they're let out.' Their conversation was interrupted by Benjamin who emerged from under the table, pushing through the folds of the cloth which hung round his face like a bonnet. 'I can climb,' he announced.

137

'I can go up a tree. I want to ride those donkeys. Why don't you come too, Fred? It's lovely. They bump you up and down and they smell nice. Where's Alice gone?'

Alice herself answered him as she came skipping into the kitchen, looking mysterious and important. 'I've gone no-where,' she said, stooping down and pulling Ben out from under the table. 'Come on out of there, Bennie. It's dinner-time. I'm going to help Mam lay the table. You can put the spoons on, can't you?' She took a white cloth out of the drawer and shook it over the table. Willie took one side of it and they spread it out straight. Alice was looking very pleased with herself and her eyes were twinkling. Willie looked at her suspiciously.

'What have you been up to all this time?' he asked. But Alice only gave a little giggle, and whispering, 'I'll tell you after,' she began to get out the plates, giving Ben a handful of spoons to lay in their places.

Fred was in such a turmoil of excitement and worry that he could hardly push his dinner down. He wanted only to be on his way; but the hands seemed to crawl round the clock face so slowly that he was sure they must have stopped altogether. Uncle John looked at him with a quizzical grin.

'Young Fred doesn't like our dumplings,' he said. 'Aunt Jen's feeding him too well, I reckon. What are we going to do with him if he doesn't eat his dinner, eh?' But Fred was not in the mood for even his uncle's teasing, and Auntie Patty, with a quick glance at his face, came to his rescue.

'They're not as good as Annie's,' she said with a warm smile at Fred. 'Your Mam makes dumplings that would feed the fairies, lad, and she'll be making some for you before you know where you are. Your Dad's gone to see her today, hasn't he?' She had arrived at the wrong reason for Fred's lack of appetite but he was grateful for her intervention and said yes, his father had gone to the hospital on the early train and would be back by six.

'Do you think they'll have dumplings for dinner there?' he asked, unable to imagine what people did in hospital except lie in bed surrounded by nurses and doctors and flowers.

'I doubt it,' said Auntie Patty, 'but I daresay they have jelly. It slips down easy, and I'm sure you can manage some now, young Fred, so you'll be having the same pudding as your Mam.'

Fred dutifully ate a plateful of jelly while Willie demolished two helpings and Ben kept hopefully asking for more. The clock struck half past one. The children were on their feet in an instant and pulling on their coats. Auntie Patty fastened Ben's gaiters with a button hook while he screamed that she was pinching his legs, and Willie danced about urging everybody to hurry up. At last they were away.

'Come round the back,' said Alice as soon as they were outside. 'I've got to fetch something.' She skipped round to the back of the bakehouse and they followed her into a small wooden shed at the bottom of the yard. Willie grumbled and protested.

'Come on, Alice. We'll be late if you don't hurry up. What d'you want in here?' Alice dived behind a pile of buckets and reappeared holding a large round object like a football, wrapped up in a brown paper bag.

'Whatever is it?' asked Fred, giving it a poke with his finger.

'Steak pudding,' said Alice gleefully. 'It's Mrs Bassenthwaite's.'

Willie sat down heavily on an upturned pot, and stared at his sister in horror. 'Alice, you can't. Whatever will Dad say when he finds out? It's Mrs Bassenthwaite's Sunday dinner.'

Alice stuck out an obstinate chin. 'We've got to get those mice out, haven't we? And we've got to keep that dog away. There weren't any bones left, see, so I had to get something else. Anyway he's not a bad dog, and he's hungry. Mrs Bassenthwaite's not hungry, she's fat. Come on, let's go.' She marched out of the shed, clasping the steak pudding firmly against her chest. 'Nobody'll know it was me that took it,' she said over her shoulder. 'Who would think of it?'

Who indeed? Fred gazed at her in awe and admiration. Willie, at a loss for words for the first time in his life, could only shake his head as they trooped up the yard. Ben was swinging on the gate where he had been waiting for them, and he wrinkled up his nose as he jumped down and took hold of Alice's coat.

'That's a nice smell,' he said. 'What you got, Alice?'

'Dog's dinner,' said Alice, without stopping. 'Come on now, we'll have to run. You run on with Willie, Bennie. Fred and me'll catch you.'

As they raced towards the Council Field, Fred explained the plan to Alice between his gasps for breath. Willie and Ben kept ahead of them in spite of Ben's frequent stumbles as he tried to make his fat little gaitered legs keep up with his brother's long loping stride. They all arrived at the Parish Hall just as the crowds of eager children were being let in.

'Keep back,' Alice whispered to Fred. 'We'll go round to the cart when it's started. See you after, Willie.' Willie nodded, and seizing Ben firmly by the shoulders guided him into the Hall. Alice and Fred crept quietly round the corner, unperceived by the circus man when he came out to shut the doors, and squatted down with their ears pressed close to the wall, listening intently. They heard nothing at first but the scuffle of feet and the scraping of chairs and the hubbub of conversation. Then came the muffled sound of the circus man's voice, and a wave of laughter from the children. At last there was a musical clatter from the piano, and the show had begun.

'Come on,' said Alice. 'Here's the scissors. We'll hide in the trees. When they all come out you undo the ropes and I'll talk to the dog.'

They stole along the side of the Hall towards the little cart standing squarely under the thorn trees with the two shaggy donkeys tethered to it, but the black dog was nowhere to be seen.

'Maybe he's inside,' whispered Alice. 'Keep quiet or he'll hear us. If he starts to bark we'll have to run.'

It was difficult to keep quiet. The snow crunched under their feet and Fred's heart was thumping so loudly in his ears that he thought all the world must hear it. But the back door of the Hall was shut, and they got safely behind the cart without disturbing anybody except one of the donkeys, which raised its head and looked at them with solemn eyes. Fred stopped to finger the knotted ropes on the cart.

'I can undo these,' he said to Alice; and suddenly he stooped, put his mouth close to the hole he had cut in the cover and called softly, 'Singleton ... are you there?'

A patter of feet answered him, and the tiniest of squeaks. 'We're here, Singleton,' whispered Fred through the hole. 'Alice and me are here. Tell Caradoc when he comes back. We'll let you out.' The back door of the Hall creaked ominously, and Alice, seizing Fred's arm, dragged him hastily away across the snow to the shelter of the thorn trees. The trees were leafless and scrubby and did not offer a great deal of cover, but they managed to conceal themselves behind a hummock of rough grass at the bottom of the tree that held the magpie's nest. Crouching close together in an attempt to keep warm, they settled down to wait. Not twenty yards away, though Alice and Fred did not know it, Puss was waiting, too – a small black shadow as still as the stone under which she lay. And in the darkest corner of the circus cart, his whiskers trembling and his heart shaking, Singleton waited alone.

An hour went by. Alice and Fred grew so cold and stiff that they could hardly feel their limbs. Fred tried putting his fingers in his mouth to warm them and Alice kept rubbing her nose. They talked in whispers and wriggled as much as they dared. At last they heard the distant chime of the Town Hall clock.

'Thank goodness,' said Alice. 'Half past three. They'll be coming out in a minute. Oh ... keep down, Fred. Here they come.'

The back door of the Parish Hall opened with a clatter, and out came the circus man with the black dog leaping round him. The donkeys raised their heads and began a little dance of welcome. The man was carrying a great tray in both hands, and he grunted savagely at the dog as it jumped up at him.

'Down, Bullseye. Get down, I say. You'll have me over.' He set the tray down behind the cart and began to undo the ropes that held the tarpaulin cover.

'Cages,' whispered Fred. 'The mice are in there. He's putting them back.' The tray was covered with a cloth, but a corner of it had slipped off and Fred could see the strong wire cages underneath. The man picked up the tray and was pushing it into the cart as children began to tumble out of the door at the other end of the Hall. They crowded round the cart, waiting eagerly for the donkeys but not daring to come too close for fear of the growling dog.

'Just you wait a minute, young ladies and young gentlemen,' said the little man hoarsely, as he leered at them over his shoulder. 'Just wait till I've packed up and I'll bring my donkeys out to you. Must pack up before it's dark.' He went back into the Hall, leaving the dog on guard and came out again a few minutes later with the little stage folded up into a flat parcel. When he had stowed it away he fastened down the ropes, blew on his hands, and turned to untie the donkeys.

'Right,' he said. 'You move off now, young ladies and young gentlemen. You can all take your turns. Threepence a go and have your money ready if you please. Stay there, Bullseye boy.' The dog lay down between the shafts of the cart, and the man shambled off leading a donkey in each hand while the children clustered after him. Fred just caught a glimpse of Willie and Ben in the crowd before they were all round the corner and out of sight.

'Now,' said Alice. 'Let me get to the dog first, and then you go.'

She scrambled to her feet, rubbing her stiff knees; and holding Mrs Bassenthwaite's Sunday pudding like a baby in her arms she walked towards the dog, calling softly to him. 'Good boy, then, good boy. Who's a hungry boy then? What about some dinner for a good boy?' Her coaxing voice went on, and before she was within a dozen yards of him the dog was on his feet, his sad bedraggled tail waving ecstatically from side to side, his eyes glistening and his mouth open.

'That dog remembers her,' thought Fred, as he watched the animal's ferocity melt away. 'He's smiling at her, I do believe.' Alice was on her knees beside Bullseye, her fingers curled in his matted hair, and the dog was licking her hand.

There was no time, however, to sit and stare. Fred stood up and made his way as quietly as he could to the back of the cart. His cold fingers were clumsy as he struggled with the knots in the ropes, but he finally pulled them undone, loosened the tarpaulin cover, and climbed inside the cart. He had to wait a few minutes for his eyes to get accustomed to the dim light that filtered through from outside. He pulled off the cloth from the tray of cages that were stacked one on top of the other, lifted each cage down, opened its door, and taking Alice's scissors from his pocket, carefully snipped the wires that bound the mice. As he worked he became aware of the awful silence in the cart. Every mouse was still. Not a claw nor a whisker stirred, not a mouse moved, even after their bonds were broken. They remained frozen, as if they had all died.

A high-pitched squeak at his feet brought him to his senses. Singleton's bright eyes, gleaming in the shadows, tried to tell him what the little mouse was unable to say. Fred suddenly realized that he himself had not spoken to the mice, and they could not yet see who he was.

'Caradoc,' he whispered, 'Caradoc, Sir. It's me, Fred. You've got to hurry. The door's open. Run, all of you. Run for your lives.'

A curious electric thrill went through the cart. There was a sudden stirring and twitching, a shiver of tails, and the mice began to squeak. Fred picked up his scissors and went on snipping urgently at the strings, setting each mouse free and talking softly all the time. It was almost impossible to recognize some of them in their bizarre costumes, and it was some time before Fred discovered Caradoc himself, imprisoned in one of the lower cages; but he found the old chief at last and released him with tender fingers. Caradoc, still dressed in top-hat and scarlet coat, bowed graciously to Fred before he took his place at the head of the line. Even so ridiculously clothed he retained his ancient dignity, and in an almost inaudible voice he spoke to Fred.

'The child, my grandson, must lead us,' he said, 'and you, a human child, have set us free. We shall meet again, perhaps. Who knows what tomorrow ...' The rest of his sentence ended in a squeak, and with an agile leap he was at the head of the procession of mice who had begun the journey out of the cart to freedom. Singleton led the way.

Almond and Arthington were the last to leave. Fred had

carefully cut loose their boxing gloves, and Arthington had been scampering up and down the ranks, bullying and cajoling those mice who were strangers to the tribe, while Almond waited, encouraging the others, until the last mouse had gone. Then they followed together. As soon as they were all out Fred climbed out himself to pull down the cover and secure the ropes before the circus man came back. Then he turned to watch the mice.

It was an extraordinary sight. Alice, still busy with the dog, saw nothing of the strange procession that wound its way across the snow towards the thorn trees, and Fred had to describe it as best he could later on. The mice were still in their circus costumes, and a motley crew of clowns, horses, acrobats and jugglers followed along a twisting track the only mouse who was not dressed up. Singleton, scampering as fast as he could, led them to the thorn trees, and began to scramble up to the magpie's nest. The others, in their brightly coloured clothes, followed him up the knobbly tree trunk, and clambering over the collection of woven twigs packed themselves tightly, one on top of another, inside the nest. It was more spacious than it looked and, although it hung high in the tree, it was well protected by its roof, and quite warm. Within a short time the mice were all inside, completely invisible. All, that is, except Almond.

His injured leg, which had been sorely strained by his performance in the circus, gave way before he had reached the trees. He fell several times, but struggled to his feet again and limped painfully on, but his movements became slower and slower until he could only just manage to crawl along the ground, and he still had a long way to go by the time the rest of the mice were tucked away in their new lodging. Fred watched in anguish as the tiny figure crept on, and was just about to dash to his rescue when there was a sudden tremendous commotion. Round the far corner of the Parish Hall at a shambling trot came the circus man leading his donkeys, followed by a crowd of shouting children. At the same moment Alice came racing from the other side of the cart. She caught Fred's hand and began pulling him away towards the trees.

'Run quick, quick,' she gasped. 'They're coming. He'll see us in a minute. Run, Fred.'

'No ... look ...' cried Fred, 'there's Almond. He can't get along. We can't leave him there. No, no, Alice, no.' He dragged his hand away, but just as he turned to run to Almond a small black thunderbolt hurled itself across his path and descended on the creeping mouse. The next instant Puss was halfway up the tree carrying Almond to safety in her mouth. The cries of the other children, the clop-clop of the donkeys' dainty hoofs and the crunching tread of the circus man's boots were close at hand. Fred and Alice took to their heels and made for the hummocks under the trees. They flung themselves down on the hard ground just as the man and his donkeys reached the cart.

It was all too much for the dog. Barking wildly, he charged in pursuit of Puss and was leaping up and down at the foot of the tree just as she scrambled beyond his reach. Balancing precariously on the roof of the magpie's nest, she dropped the mouse inside and jumped for a higher branch of the tree. The slender branch, made brittle by the frost, snapped, and Puss fell, her claws clutching at empty air, down, down towards the open jaws of the slavering dog below.

Bullseye was very full of Mrs Bassenthwaite's steak pudding, and although he instinctively gave chase at the sight of any cat, his reactions in his replete condition were slower than usual. A low sweet call from behind the hummock added to his confusion.

'Good boy, then,' came Alice's soft coaxing voice. 'Good old boy, good dog.' For a second he hesitated and turned his head to listen. A second was all Puss needed. As she fell, her body twisted gracefully and she landed on her feet a few inches from the dog just as he looked away. In one swift movement she sprang up and was climbing the next thorn tree before he could collect his wits. This time she made no mistake. She travelled sure-footed along the line of trees, leaping from branch to branch, while the dog followed her on the ground barking in frustrated fury.

'What's to do, Bullseye?' shouted his master above the uproar. 'Stop your noise, now, do. Cats, is it? After our friends, I don't doubt, but they're all stowed away safe, boy. Now, young ladies and young gentlemen, be off with you if you please. You've had a good day and it's time me and my donkeys was on our way. You won't forget the Mouse Circus, will you? Dancing mice, fighting mice, mice playing in a band. Never seen anything like it. We'll be back next year, sure enough. Trust Jem Leary.' His harsh voice intoning the circus cries brought the dog back to his side. He tied the donkeys loosely to the cart, picked up the shafts, bent his back, and shuffled away across the Council Field, the black dog loping beside him. The crowd of children followed the strange little circus across the field, and when they reached the road, broke up into groups and went home for tea. Alice and Fred watched the disappearing cart until it was out of sight, and turned to meet Willie and Ben who were coming towards them across the deserted field.

'Ben wanted to say goodbye to the donkeys,' said Willie, 'so we went along with them for a bit.' He cocked an eye at the magpie's nest in the thorn tree. 'Are they all right up there?'

Fred nodded without speaking. Excitement and terror and relief had worn him out. Alice stood shading her eyes with her hand, looking along the road where the Mouse Circus had gone.

'He wasn't a bad dog, that,' she murmured softly to herself. 'Not a bad dog at all.'

147

18

It was surprisingly comfortable in the magpie's nest. The mice, packed closely together, kept each other warm, though they were not so cramped as to prevent their moving about a little. Singleton had worked his way up from the bottom until he reached Almond's side, and curled up contentedly with his head under his guardian's chin. As soon as it was dark Caradoc took up a commanding position on the fork of a twig just below the roof of the nest, and began to address the company.

'We are, I think, all here, including our new friends. There is a long night before us, which is fortunate because there is a great deal to be done. Our first task is to divest ourselves of this appalling raiment. Each must assist the other. The garments are close-fitting and the threads are fine but strong; and tooth and claw will have to work for several hours before we are wholly free.' His own top hat was by now set crookedly on his head and bobbed about at a rakish angle as he talked. He looked round thoughtfully at his people. The strangers who had joined them were both bewildered and impressed by his antique manner of speaking, and did not find it easy to understand; but they followed the example of the others and started to gnaw and drag at the threads that tied on their costumes. Before long the nest began to look as though it were strewn with confetti. Tiny shreds of brightly-coloured cloth were scattered amongst the twigs, and within a few hours all that remained of the beautifully fashioned miniature garments were little bits of tattered rag. It was hard work, and the efforts of the mice made a great rustling in the nest, which swayed and rocked alarmingly in the branches as they struggled on. At last

every mouse was free of clothes and strings, and Caradoc
once more commanded silence and attention.

'We shall have to remain here for the present,' he said.
'The boy Fred, who saved our lives, assured me that further
help would come to us. Nevertheless it may be some time.
As you are aware, humans wake by day and sleep at night.
A curious habit. We therefore cannot expect the boy and
his cousins to come to our rescue until another day has
dawned, and I doubt if our friend Puss can do a great deal
without their help.' A shudder went through the group of

strangers at the mention of Puss, and Caradoc looked ruefully at them. 'I am unable to convince you of her good-
will, I see. Perhaps time will tell. Meanwhile we must wait
as patiently as we can.'

It was Janus who answered him. 'Caradoc, Sir. There were
people in the Hall after we got away. There were lights in
the windows and I could hear singing. They might have left
something to eat, you know. Some of the children who came
to the circus were eating biscuits. I saw them. I could take a
foraging party to see what we could find. Everybody's
hungry, Sir, particularly the little ones. There must be
crumbs about, surely.'

Janus's voice was desperate with hunger. The mice had
not eaten since morning, and after all their hard work they
had become preoccupied with the desire for food. A dozen
of them squeaked in approval and offered to accompany
Janus in the search for crumbs. One of the first to offer, to
everyone's surprise, was young Calverley. Janus hesitated,
and Arthington grunted suspiciously.

'What's he up to now?' he muttered. 'Wouldn't trust
him as far as I could see him. Much better keep an eye on
him here.'

But Calverley stood up straight and turning to Caradoc
looked him in the eye.

'Sir, I have learnt a lot, these last few days; and so have
my brothers and cousins. Give us a chance, Sir, please.'

Caradoc regarded him gravely for a moment without
speaking. Then he said, 'I think, young man, that Janus
may be glad of your company. Seven of you from Otley, together with the Follifoots, and Arthington of course, will
be enough. I need not remind you that Janus is in command.'
He glanced from Calverley to Arthington's disapproving
face, and in spite of his weariness his eyes twinkled with
amusement. 'Go with care. We shall await your return with
hopeful hearts.'

Janus scrambled up to the edge of the nest and looked out into the night. Signalling to the others, he climbed cautiously out and descended the tree trunk backwards, clinging to the bark with his claws and balancing himself with his tail. His companions followed, one at a time. Arthington brought up the rear, and Caradoc found time to speak quietly to him before he left.

'Do not be too hard on them,' he said gently. 'They are young and headstrong, I know, but they are not all foolishness.' Arthington was unconvinced, but he bowed dutifully to his chief and followed the others down the tree.

Janus's sight was so acute that he very easily found the track that led to the back of the Parish Hall. He covered the ground in swift darting rushes, and his companions scampered after him following the swing of his tail. There was a gap under the outer door quite big enough for them to creep through, and the inner door to the Hall had been left ajar. After that their noses told them all they needed to know. Joyfully they raced round the floor of the Hall, squeaking with delight. There were crumbs everywhere; broken biscuits, apple cores, bits of cake and the fragments of sandwiches. It was a feast indeed, and Janus had some difficulty in gathering his excited band together.

'Now look,' he said. 'There's plenty for all of us. We can eat a bit first – not too much, mind – and then we'll carry all we can back to the others. We can come back for more if we need.' He was desperately hungry himself, and even while he was speaking he began to nibble at a piece of sugary cake. It was delicious. For the next few minutes the mice ran ecstatically about, filling themselves with crumbs, until at last Janus called a halt. Reluctantly the mice gathered round him, snatching a few more delicacies on the way.

'That's enough,' said Janus, cleaning his whiskers with his paws. 'Now pick up as much as you can hold in your mouths ... fill your cheeks ... and we'll carry it to the others. And no swallowing it on the way, mind. Keep close after me. We don't want anybody to get lost.'

It was a cheerful procession back to the magpie's nest, and the welcome the explorers received when they arrived was most rewarding. Janus and his party bestowed their booty on their hungry companions, and set off at once to collect some more. Back and forth they went in the dark until all the mice were satisfied, and squeaks of pleasure greeted their return each time. After their fifth journey Caradoc raised his claw to restrain the excitement. 'That is enough,' he said. 'It was bravely done, and we are all grateful. But it is almost morning, and time for us to rest. Who knows what tomorrow may bring?'

Janus was flushed with triumph at the success of his expedition and for once paid no attention to Caradoc's signal for dismissal. Forgetting his usual caution in his excitement, he pleaded for one more excursion. 'Some of the children are still hungry,' he said, 'and there will be no chance in the daylight.' So against his better judgement Caradoc gave way.

The little band set off once more. By this time they were all so pleased with themselves that they danced blithely across the snow towards the Parish Hall, looking forward to another little feast on their own before they carried the last load of provisions back to the tribe. Young Calverley, who had learnt a lot but not quite enough, forgot his promise to Caradoc and with a bounding leap scampered ahead of Janus, eager to be first into the Parish Hall.

Three yards ahead, on the step where the circus dog had been lying, he came face to face with a pair of glowing eyes, two pricked ears, twitching whiskers, and the lash of a tail : for one brief moment he thought it was Puss.

But he was wrong. It was not Puss at all, but a great grey tomcat with silvery fur and scarred ears and ferocious teeth, and muscles of steel drawn back for a spring.

Janus uttered a piercing shriek of warning. 'Run! Run for your lives! Scatter, all of you.' He swung sideways, dodging from side to side, turning in his tracks like a hare; and the other mice who had immediately broken ranks were at the same instant scattered all over the snow, weaving their way back and forth to the shelter of the thorn trees.

'The young fool,' muttered Arthington glancing back as he raced hither and thither. And suddenly he stopped short and stared in disbelief at Calverley. 'Oh my,' he gasped aloud. 'He's trying to draw him off.'

There was a clear run to the gap under the door between the dodging mouse and the grey tomcat that waited to pounce, but Calverley did not take it. Instead he swerved and began to run along the side of the Parish Hall, leading his pursuer away from the escaping mice. He was an easy prey, his brown fur clearly visible against the snow. The cat galloped after him, and stretching out a paw, knocked him off his feet. Then it stood back and waited for him to move, so that the game could go on. Calverley opened his mouth and uttered a series of pitiful shrieks, then got to his feet and began to run again, blindly. Once more the steel grey paw came out and felled him with a blow. The little mouse, whimpering in terror, gave himself up for lost. The cat sat down and watched him with his head on one side. The rest of the party had regained the safety of the nest and were trying to tell Caradoc what had happened, all talking at once. Only Arthington remained outside, and he crouched with closed eyes, unable to look, while Calverley lay helpless, his rash heroism forgotten, hoping for a quick death.

A melodious thrilling cry broke the silence of the night. It was a love call, sweet, shrill, and for the grey tomcat, quite irresistible. He lifted his head and stood, tail lashing, whiskers vibrating, with his back to Calverley.

A small black shape emerged from the shadows, and Puss

came treading softly over the snow. She rubbed her head under the grey cat's chin, then danced lightly away with another wooing call. He followed her, flattening his silvery ears and uttering little crows of recognition. Puss waited for him, arching her back, and they stepped round each other in a strange slow dance. Gradually she led him farther and farther away from the spot where Calverley lay; and Arthington, who had at last dared to open his eyes, watched them disappear together into the dark.

Gasping for breath he raced across to the Parish Hall where Calverley lay trembling against the wall.

'You prize young idiot,' he said roughly. 'Come on. I'll take you back. Get up and run.' He pushed his nose into the young mouse's side and gave him a sharp but oddly affectionate nip on the ear. Calverley shuddered and sighed; then shook himself, staggered to his feet, and ran uncertainly beside Arthington to the thorn trees. 'Up you go,' grunted Arthington. They climbed, one behind the other, and appeared over the edge of the magpie's nest just as the rest of the mice had given up all hope of their return.

Calverley was too shaken to say anything in reply to Caradoc's questioning, but Arthington described what had happened. Caradoc listened gravely, and when Arthington had finished speaking, turned to the group of strangers. 'Perhaps you will one day be persuaded that there are cats and cats,' he said. 'Once more Puss has come to the rescue of our people. Such an ally is beyond the price of pearls.'

'What I don't understand, though,' said Arthington, who was lying close to Calverley with his chin resting protectively on the younger mouse's neck, 'is how she happened to be there at the time. I don't think it was because of us, though when she saw us in trouble of course she came to help. But the grey cat didn't seem surprised to see her. He seemed almost to be waiting for her, out there on the step.'

Caradoc gave him the ghost of a smile. 'It was a fortunate

accident. Puss's fur is jet black, but have you not observed,' he said, 'that the kittens all have silvery paws?'

[19]

Fred and his cousins had lingered long after all the other children had made their way home, and it was getting late. Walking home in the gathering darkness they went, one behind the other, like a trail of fieldmice. Willie, who had brought a small lantern with him and had managed to beg a light from one of the early arrivals for choir-practice, led the way; and Ben, holding with both hands on to Alice's coat, stumped along at the back. Everybody else had gone, and it seemed a long way, following the bobbing lantern, across the Sally Lunn and along the road to the Square, before they saw the lights of the bakehouse. Benjamin kept his spirits up by chanting to nobody in particular.

'I go this way and that way,' he sang to himself in a tuneless undertone, 'this way and that way and over the hill. Threepence a go. Mouses, mouses, come out of your houses. Trust Jem Leary.'

Under the cover of Ben's singing Fred said to Willie, 'We've got to get them back to the snow house, quick. They can't stay in that tree.'

'I've been thinking about that,' said Willie. 'We could take the barrow from the shed ... or we could get one of the sacks – that'd be better – they went off in a bag so they might as well come back in one. We could go for them tonight, maybe, when everybody's asleep. Could you get out, Fred?'

Alice's voice came floating through the darkness. 'That's daft,' she said. 'We'd never manage without a light and somebody's sure to see us. They'll be all right till tomorrow.

What's the matter with Sunday morning when we go to Chapel? I can easy push a sack under my coat. We can turn off at the corner and nobody'll know we haven't been if we go and get them quick and get in at the end for the blessing hymn.' She gave one of her customary little skips as she settled the matter. Her cheerful flouting of the moral code in which they had been brought up filled Fred and Willie with a fearful admiration. Not only was she capable of stealing steak puddings but she was now proposing to play truant from Chapel on Sunday morning. The wrath of God, thought Fred, would surely descend on them before long. But the thought of the mice waiting hopefully and patiently for rescue from the tree tops overcame his scruples. By the time they reached the bakehouse door everything had been

arranged, and they only had to wait until the next morning before the mice would be safely back in their ice-palace.

It was long past tea time when they crept apprehensively into the kitchen, expecting a scolding from Auntie Patty for being so late. To Fred's surprise and delight he found his father sitting by the fire, his hat perched on the back of his head, deep in conversation with Uncle John.

'Why, Dad,' he cried, 'I didn't know you were coming. You never said.'

'I came seeking you, young Fred,' said his father with a rueful grin. 'Fine time of night to be coming home, I must say. We were just going to send the bellman after you. Thought you must all have gone off with your precious circus. And we've eaten all your tea.' He twinkled at

the children, and his eyes were very bright. Fred grinned back at him with pleasure, while his cousins all began to talk at once.

'I'm hungry,' proclaimed Ben, as his mother peeled off his coat and scarf and sat him on the floor to unbutton his gaiters. 'Hungry, hungry, hungry. Are those mice and donkeys having their tea, I wonder?'

'I should think they've had it long since,' said Auntie Patty, lifting Ben on to his chair and spreading treacle on his bread. 'It's nearly supper-time.' Fred thought sadly of the hungry mice marooned in the magpie's nest with not a crumb between them, knowing nothing of the forays that Janus and his gallant band would make that night. He said very little, though Willie and Alice chattered incessantly about the Mouse Circus, and Ben climbed down from his chair as soon as he had finished his tea and galloped about the room riding imaginary donkeys. The noise and warmth in the bakehouse, so comforting after the cold walk home in the dark, made him feel sleepy. Auntie Patty caught Ben in the middle of one of his gallops and carried him off to bed. Fred slid down on to the hearthrug and leaned against Dad's knees, his eyes growing heavy. His father looked down at him and scratched the top of his head with the stem of his pipe.

'Wake up, lad. It's time I took you home. How would you fancy staying with Willie and Alice for a couple of nights next week, young Fred?'

'Stay here? Do you mean sleep here?' Fred sat up with a puzzled frown. 'What for, Dad?'

'I have to go away for a day or two,' said Dad. 'They want me at the hospital for some tests, and to see the doctors about Mam. Aunt Jen's coming with me – she wants to visit some cousins of hers in Leeds. So your Auntie Patty says you can stay here and sleep in with Willie till I'm back. How about it, eh?'

Fred looked a little alarmed at the prospect. He had never slept away from home in his life, and could not imagine what 'sleeping in with Willie' would be like. The thought of Dad going to the hospital that had swallowed up his mother for so many months was even more alarming, and he stared at his father with anxious eyes. 'You won't stay there, Dad? You won't go to bed there, will you?'

'Not a chance. I'll be back in a day or two, don't you fret.' Dad gave Fred an affectionate poke with his pipe. Willie was marching up and down in excitement, and Alice skipped with pleasure.

'That'll be fine, Fred. You'll be here for breakfast and we'll all come back from school for tea and you don't have to go home for supper and we can all talk in bed. You can see the snow house from the upstairs windows, Fred. Maybe you can stay here always and not go home at all. When's he coming, Uncle Fred?'

Laughing at her eagerness, Fred's father tugged at Alice's dark hair. 'I'm off on Tuesday or Wednesday, and I expect I'll be back Saturday afternoon. Then you'll come home to me, young Fred, full of Auntie Patty's curranty, as fat as a suet pudding.'

'That reminds me,' said Uncle John suddenly, while Fred sat thinking about it all, 'talking of suet puddings. I wonder what Mrs Bassenthwaite will think of her Sunday dinner?'

There was a moment's awful silence. Willie stopped short, staring open-mouthed at his father. Fred's face went scarlet and he hung his head to conceal his burning cheeks and to avoid his uncle's eyes. Alice, though taken by surprise, was quick to recover her wits, and raised wide innocent eyes to her father's face. Only her fingers, nervously pleating her skirt, betrayed her guilty anxiety.

'What's wrong with her Sunday dinner, Dad? She always has steak pudding. Lily likes it.'

'Well,' said Uncle John, 'I only hope Lily will like the one she has tomorrow. It's one of mine. When I took them all out tonight I couldn't find Mrs Bassenthwaite's anywhere. The label must have come off somehow. I had one or two made ready to sell, so I've had to put one of those aside for her. It's never happened before, and it's been bothering me the whole evening. I reckon the mice have been in ... two legged mice, most likely. It's not good for trade.'

He gave Alice a long deep look, and the ghost of a smile hovered on his mouth. Alice would not meet his eyes, but twirled about on her toes, and with a little toss of her head said in a jaunty voice, 'Lucky old Lily Bassenthwaite. Your steak puddings are much better than her Mam's.'

She danced away, and Uncle John shook his head and exchanged glances with Fred's father. Dad got up and pulled Fred to his feet.

'That's settled then. Time to go, lad. Aunt Jen'll be coming out to look for us before long. Say good night to your Auntie Patty,' she had just come down after settling Ben, 'and we'll be on our way. Good night all. Don't be late in the morning.' He grinned round at the family, took Fred's hand, and they went out together. Alice and Willie were soon sent up to bed, and Uncle John drew his chair closer to the fire.

'Now I wonder,' he said thoughtfully, as he raked the coals with the poker, 'just what young Alice did with that steak pudding?'

Young Fred slept fitfully that night. In his dreams he found himself either sleeping in the magpie's nest with his pockets full of mice, rocked by the wind in the treetops, or in a narrow bed with Willie talking into his ear and Ben galloping over the pillows. Every now and then he woke, staring into the dark. 'Puss,' he murmured, half asleep, 'where are you, Puss?' But she did not come.

She came, in fact, in the early dawn when at last Fred was

deeply asleep. She purred into his ear, but he did not stir and, looking into his exhausted face, she went quietly away up the ladder to the loft, and lay down in the basket to console her kittens.

[20]

Sunday was a bright clear day. The greyness had gone from the sky. The night's sharp frost had brought back the sparkle to the snow, and another light fall had eliminated the children's footprints and freshened the white covering of the Square.

Young Fred, dressed in his Sunday suit with its hard white collar that dug uncomfortably into his neck, set off soon after breakfast for the bakehouse, his collection penny and a little bag of peppermints stowed in his pocket. As he opened the kitchen door Puss slipped out ahead of him, but before he could catch her up she had vanished round the corner.

Ben was not old enough to go to Chapel, and he was playing with his Noah's Ark on the floor when Fred arrived. 'Look, Fred,' he said, pushing it backwards and forwards across the carpet. 'I could sail it on the water and my pigs and sheep could go sailing far away. But there's no water.'

'There will be,' said Auntie Patty, 'when this snow melts. More than we bargained for, I reckon.' Ben looked up hopefully.

'Will my Noah's Ark sail on it then?'

'I daresay,' said Auntie Patty, going to the foot of the stairs to call to Willie and Alice. They came clattering down and erupted into the kitchen, and Willie made straight for the door.

'Late again, Fred,' he said impatiently, about to disappear at once; but Auntie Patty seized him by the back of his coat.

'He's not in the least late,' she said, with a glance at the clock. 'Stop stamping about, Willie, do. And stand still, Alice, while I get these tangles out of your hair. I shouldn't think it's seen a brush since you got up. You look very smart this morning, Fred. Willie, your bootlace is undone. Now then, you're just about ready. Mind how you go, and see if you can stay tidy till you get to Chapel.' All these admonitions were softened by Auntie Patty's friendly smile, and when the children finally tumbled out of the house she stood in the doorway to watch them jog-trotting across the Square, their feet crunching the crisp new snow.

They made their way to the crossroads where they intended to slip away to the Sally Lunn. Little knots of children, muffled up against the cold, were trudging along ahead of them on their way to Chapel. There was a special service for children before the main morning service on Sundays. It lasted about half an hour, after which most of the children repaired to the back of the Chapel to make scrapbooks and listen to Bible stories read to them by the stout lady who had played the piano for the Mouse Circus. At intervals she would depart to play the harmonium for the hymns, and if the babble of children's voices grew louder it was usually drowned by the singing of the congregation. Auntie Patty usually brought Ben along to join the others at the back while she attended morning service, and several other infants came too. It was a very convenient arrangement all round.

It presented problems, however, for Willie and Alice and Fred that particular Sunday. 'I couldn't get into the shed for a sack,' said Alice, as they hurried along. 'Dad was in there stacking up boxes and I didn't dare go – not after the steak pudding. But I've got four big pockets, two in my coat and

162

two in my skirt, and Willie's got four. How many've you got, Fred?'

Fred anxiously patted his clothes. 'Two in my coat and two in my trousers, and three in my jacket. They're not very big though.'

'Well,' said Alice, 'we'll just have to manage. The mice'll have to squash down. Some can go in my straw bag.'

'It wouldn't have been any use getting a sack, anyway,' said Willie. 'There's no place to put it, and how could we take a sack to Chapel?' Fred stared at him in amazement, and he continued, 'We'll have to take the mice to Chapel. We can't get back to the snow house first because we'll meet Mam and Ben and maybe lots of other people and they'll find out we haven't been. We shall have to keep them in our pockets till we can take them back when nobody's looking.'

The prospect of sitting in Chapel with his pockets full of mice was almost too much for Fred, but Alice produced a comforting answer to his protests. 'We can slip out when they start the last hymn. Nobody'll notice. We can run quick to the snow house and put them in, and when Mam brings Ben along she'll think we've just gone on ahead. We'll go back later and take them something to eat. They'll be right starving by then.'

Fred was extremely dubious about the possibility of fitting so many mice into all their pockets without suffocating them, but there was nothing else for it. The children had reached the crossroads and there was not a minute to be lost. Turning right instead of left, they sped away towards the Sally Lunn. Under the thorn trees they stood breathless and irresolute, staring up at the magpie's nest, uncertain what to do next.

'You'd better go up, young Fred,' Willie said. 'They know you. Alice and me'll give you a hump up.'

He bent his back and Fred climbed on to it and began to

163

struggle up the tree trunk. Barking his knees and his elbows and clinging on with frozen fingers he managed to reach the lowest branch of the thorn tree and swing his legs over so that he could sit astride it. Above him hung the untidy mass of twigs in which the mice had spent the night. He looked up, calling softly, 'Caradoc, Caradoc, Sir. It's me, Fred. Can you climb down, all of you? Me and Willie and Alice, we've come to take you home.' He waited, knowing the mice would be cautious in showing themselves, and then climbed down the tree and stood at the bottom without another word. Willie, impatient as ever, was about to speak; but Fred, with unaccustomed authority, lifted his hand to stop him.

It seemed to the children that they waited for hours in the frosty silence, though it was in reality only a minute or two before there was a rustling and a stirring above their heads, and two round ears and a pointed nose appeared over the edge of the magpie's nest. Fred caught his breath. 'Come on down,' he called. 'Come down here to me, Caradoc.'

He could not make out, at that distance, which of them had ventured into view, but as the mice made their zig-zag descent of the tree trunk he saw that it was Arthington who was leading the way, followed closely by his brothers, young Calverley, and the Cleveland-Tontines. The rest came down too quickly for him to recognize them, but he stooped and gathered them up in his hands, stowing them carefully in his pockets. Alice and Willie followed his example, and soon all their pockets were bulging with mice. Fred watched closely enough to make sure that he had Caradoc, Almond and Singleton in his own keeping. There were a few strangers among them, more nervous than the others, and a number of very young babies that clung tightly to their mothers' fur as they made the perilous journey down the tree. Fred began to wonder rather desperately if there would be room for them all. They were crushed uncomfortably together, so close that they could scarcely breathe.

'At least they can't wriggle,' muttered Willie grimly as he pushed more and more of the little creatures into his already over-crowded pockets. 'We'll never get them all in, Fred, I reckon. There's too many.'

Alice had emptied the straw bag that held her hymn book, a packet of humbugs and a clean handkerchief, and filled it full of mice. Regretfully she abandoned the humbugs, and spread her handkerchief over the heap of furry bodies in the bag. But there were still a dozen mice crouching in the snow at their feet, and the children looked despairingly at each other.

Suddenly Alice gave one of her excited little skips, joggling the mice in her pockets and making them squeak in alarm. She pulled off her woollen cap, tucked the remaining mice inside it, and fitted it carefully back on her head. Tiny claws clung to the fine strands of her hair and prickled her scalp, making her shiver. 'They tickle,' she said with a nervous giggle, 'but they're all in. Let's go.' Picking up her hymn book and the straw bag she led the way back across the Sally Lunn. Fred and Willie followed, running as quickly as they dared, and the mice endured the shaking and bumping as patiently as they could.

'Who knows, indeed,' thought Almond ruefully to himself, 'what tomorrow may bring?'

It was not until the children had disappeared that Puss detached herself from the spiky branch of a neighbouring tree and made her own way home. Ben would probably have seen her from the first, but Ben was not there.

Fred never forgot that Sunday morning in Chapel. He and his cousins stole quietly in during the second verse of the last hymn, and took their places, flushed and uncomfortable, amongst the other children near the back. One or two of their schoolfellows looked curiously at them.

'Playing truant, eh?' muttered John Henry Bly in Willie's ear. 'You wait till your Mam finds out.'

But Willie was bigger than John Henry and was able to subdue him with a ferocious glare. As the last notes of the harmonium wheezed into silence, all the children closed their hymn books with a slap and moved away to the back, jostling through the adults who were already coming in for the main service. Benjamin, escaping from Auntie Patty's restraining hand, ran to join them, his clear voice ringing above the subdued chatter and the shuffling of feet.

'I can do that puzzle with a donkey on it, can't I, Willie? It's a brown donkey not a white one though, with cows and horses and a baby. I haven't got a baby in my farm. Can I have a humbug please, Alice?'

'Shush,' said Alice, tucking her hymn book under her arm and carrying her straw bag with great care. 'Come on, Ben. I'll find that puzzle for you. Don't shout, though.' She led him away, while he repeated in a piercing whisper, 'Can I have a humbug out of your bag, please?'

Alice waited until she was quite sure Auntie Patty was out of earshot before she whispered back, 'I haven't got any humbugs, Bennie.' Looking down at her little brother's puckered face she added hastily, 'Fred's got some peppermints, though. Lovely white hot ones. We'll all have one in

166

a minute.' Fred's peppermints, which he had fortunately kept in his hand when he emptied his pockets to make room for the mice, were warm and damp and sticky. Alice took them from him and popped two into Ben's mouth. They were hot and fierce and Ben had to keep his mouth open to cool his tongue while he gasped for breath.

For the next half hour, while stories were read and the children played and the service went on, Willie and Alice and Fred stood stiffly about, unable to sit down for fear of squashing the mice. Willie shuffled restlessly from one foot to the other. Alice stood at a table clutching her straw bag and helping Ben with his puzzle. Fred pretended to concentrate on his scrapbook while he tried to conceal the movement of his bulging pockets which rose and fell with the laboured breathing of the mice. At last the stout lady went up to the harmonium to play the closing hymn, and Willie shuffled closer to Fred.

'Now,' he muttered, 'as soon as she starts we'll go, Fred. Mam'll bring Ben.' He looked at his little brother. 'We're going to have a race to the snow house, Bennie, Alice and Fred and me. Who d'you reckon will win? You stay here and wait for Mam.'

'Mouses, mouses,' Ben began to chant, but Alice clapped her gloved hand across his mouth. 'You watch us,' she whispered to him. 'We're going to creep out like mouses, Fred and Willie and me. Just you watch.'

Under cover of the hymn singing they went quietly and sedately out of Chapel, while Ben stared after them with his mouth wide open. Then, throwing both caution and consideration for the comfort of the mice to the winds, they raced across the Square. They arrived breathless, and began at once to shed their burdens. Mice poured out of their pockets like a waterfall, and disappeared through the windows and doors of the snow house with a flash of whiskers and a flicker of tails. There was not a squeak left in them, and in the dark interior of the snow house there was complete silence.

The children stood still for a moment, speechless with relief. Then suddenly the tension broke. Aunty Patty and Ben appeared at the far corner, and Willie turned to meet Ben as he broke away from his mother and came running across the Square. He seized the little boy by the coat and swung him round and round until he was dizzy, and tumbled into a heap on the snow, rosy and laughing. Fred began to caper madly round the snow house, shouting and waving his arms. Alice flung her cap into the air and twirled round in triumph.

'What's got into you all?' said Auntie Patty. 'You look like a lot of dervishes. It's no way to behave on a Sunday.'

Her reproof calmed the children's wild excitement. Alice picked Ben up, set him on his feet and brushed him down. 'Go back,' sang Ben cheerfully at the top of his voice. 'Go back to your houses, mouses.' But nobody took any notice of him, and they all went home to their Sunday dinner.

'See you after, Fred,' called Alice. Young Fred waved his hand, and went off by himself to The Sundial.

[22]

The next few days passed uneventfully for Fred, except for Aunt Jen's sudden determination to turn The Sundial upside down in an access of scouring and scrubbing and polishing. He hardly dared set foot in the house when he came home from school in case his boots sullied the spotless kitchen floor. Puss retreated to the loft and rarely appeared downstairs. Fred's father protested mildly once or twice.

'Really, Jen, there's no need. Anybody would think the Queen was coming to tea.' But all he got in response was a sniff from Aunt Jen and a short answer.

'Maybe she is . . .' So, with a shake of his head and a rueful grin at Fred, he, too, retreated, into the shop, and said no more. Young Fred spent most of his time with his cousins, and both his father and his aunt seemed too preoccupied to question what he did.

More than a week went by, and there had been no fresh snow. The ground was gripped in ice and the sky had a leaden look. The children had made a long slide in the Square by the snow house, and they polished it with their boots as they slid along its glassy length, bruising their elbows and knees every time they fell on the hard shiny surface.

'Weather's on the change, I reckon,' said Uncle John, glancing up at the heavy sky as he stood in the bakehouse doorway watching the children's games. But they had grown too used to the winter to believe him, and even Willie had ceased to think that it might one day come to an end.

They went to the snow house every day, posting crusts and apples and biscuits, saved from their lunch boxes, through the windows; but the mice did not come outside even for the chocolate Alice tried to tempt them with. They had grown wise and wary, and seemed to have returned to their old shy secret ways. Only an occasional squeak, a few tiny tracks in the snow, and what Willie called the 'crumby smell', betrayed their presence. Fred was both disappointed and relieved. Mindful of what Puss had said, he knew the mice were safer if they remained hidden, though he longed for a conversation with them. Alice, who liked to organize people's lives and was happiest when she was cherishing those in need, grew a little bored with their independence.

Willie always had so many things to think about that he did not worry about the mice's welfare, though he never failed to supply them with food.

Fred had almost forgotten the proposed stay with his cousins, but the following Tuesday morning his father closed the shop and said goodbye to his son when he set off for school. 'I'll drop your things in at your uncle's before we go,' he said. 'Enjoy yourself, lad, and don't eat too much curranty. I'll be home on Saturday.' He rumpled Fred's hair and gave him a friendly poke. Aunt Jen bent down and pecked his cheek, tucking his scarf into his coat.

'Now be a good boy and don't catch cold,' she said, as if freedom from colds were a part of good behaviour.

Fred turned back to his father and said anxiously, 'What about Puss, Dad? Will she be all right, all alone?'

His father gave him a reassuring grin. 'I reckon so. Your Uncle John's coming in to feed her and the kits; and what makes you think she'll be alone? Haven't you heard that gentleman friend of hers singing his love-songs all this week? If I know Puss, she'll be out half the night. And then we'll have another crop of kittens to look after. But that's all right. They're good company. Don't you fret about our Puss.'

Aunt Jen gave vent to a last sniff of disapproval. The private life of cats, she considered, should be confined to the dutiful destruction of mice; and the private lives of mice were beyond her comprehension. Fred, however, was relieved and comforted by his father's remarks. They explained Puss's long absences and her reluctance to talk to him. She was clearly otherwise occupied, with more immediate and important affairs than human conversation. But he did not doubt that she would find time to keep an eye on the welfare of her friends.

When he came home from school he went to the bakehouse instead of to the familiar bedroom in The Sundial.

171

Auntie Patty made him feel warm and welcome; but he was still apprehensive when he went up at bedtime to Willie's and Ben's bedroom. The feather bed that he was to share with Willie was large and inviting and comfortable; but it was not until he had explored the small canvas bag which held his possessions that he really felt secure. Clean underclothes and a nightshirt had been neatly packed for him by Aunt Jen. Tucked away at the bottom of the bag was the little wooden mouse that bounced up and down on its spring. Dad had put it in, he knew. He hid it under his pillow in Willie's bed, and when he went to sleep his hand curved round it; a companion in his dreams.

[23]

'Look Willie! Look Fred, look! It's raining ... it's raining *stair rods*!'

Ben's voice shattered the morning. He was kneeling in his nightshirt on the chest of drawers by the bedroom window, holding the curtains apart with his two fat hands, and staring out into the Square. Fred swam up into consciousness from the sleepy warmth of Willie's feather bed. He rubbed his eyes, not understanding what Ben was talking about. There was a curious drumming sound in his ears, a hissing on the window pane, and the noise of flowing water as if somebody had left all the taps running.

All at once Ben began to cry. 'It's gone,' he sobbed. 'The snow house has gone and it's all spoilt and it isn't there any more. Where's my snow house gone to? It's all broken and bent, Fred. Can't you mend it?'

Suddenly sick with fear, Fred scrambled out of bed, dragging the bedclothes on to the floor after him, leaving Willie protesting vigorously. 'Hey, Fred, it's cold. What's going on then? Where are you off to, Fred?' Turning over, he tried to heave the blankets back over his shoulders, but at Fred's cry of dismay he sat up and staggered after him to the bedroom window. Together they stared, speechless, open-mouthed, and suddenly wide awake, at the disastrous scene outside.

While they slept, the whole world had changed. The hard-packed snow that had covered the Square for months with a sparkling white carpet was rapidly being destroyed by the onslaught of the rain which must have been falling all night. It was fierce heavy rain that descended in a continuous downpour like a curtain through which it was difficult to see. The snow had lost all its crystal beauty. It was no longer white, but steely grey, and pitted into holes by the merciless attack of a thousand spears. The roof gutters were over-flowing, and water streamed down the pipes and windows of the houses in the Square and swirled in dirty pools on the ground below. The rain fell so heavily that it bounced up again from the puddles like a host of jumping jacks. Fred rubbed his fists over the bedroom window in a desperate effort to see across the Square, but it was like looking through a waterfall. He could just make out the snow house, and saw that it had already become shrunken and misshapen, and seemed to be disappearing beneath an enormous lake.

Ben's shoulders shook with his loud sobs, and Fred beat his hands on the window-pane in helpless misery. He wished he had never left The Sundial. 'If only I'd been at home,' he thought. 'Puss would have wakened me and told me about the rain and we could have saved the mice in time. The mice,' he cried aloud in despair. 'They'll all be drowned and lost, all of them, Caradoc and Almond and Singleton and all. Oh Willie, Willie, whatever shall we do?'

'Do?' said Alice, as she ran into their bedroom with her patchwork dressing-gown flying behind her like a brightly-coloured flag. 'Why, go out and get them, of course. Stop crying, Bennie, and come on downstairs quick.' She swung Ben off the chest of drawers, seized him by the hand, and raced downstairs while he ran gasping along with her. Willie and Fred followed closely, barefooted and in their nightshirts, and they all rushed headlong into the kitchen where Auntie Patty was stirring the porridge on the hob.

'Good gracious me,' she exclaimed in astonishment at their sudden appearance. 'Willie, whatever do you think you're doing now? And where do you think you're going in your nightshirt with nothing on your feet? Come back here this minute.'

Willie had charged straight to the kitchen door, over-taking Alice and Ben; but his mother's voice was so un-usually severe that he paused, with his hand on the latch. Alice stopped for a moment halfway across the room. 'It's the mice in the snow house, Mam,' she said, throwing caution and secrets to the wind. 'They'll all get drowned dead in the flood and we've got to get them out.' She danced with impatience, but her mother, abandoning the porridge, marched firmly over to the kitchen door, turned Willie round by the collar of his nightshirt and brought him back to the hearthrug by the fire.

'It's not only mice that will be getting drowned,' she said definitely. 'I must say I'm surprised at you, Willie – and you too, Alice. What you can be thinking of, I don't know. Here's Fred not long got over bronchitis, and his Dad coming home on Saturday. And Ben, ready to follow you out into the rain in his nightshirt, not knowing any better. Not one of you dressed or decent, and all this talk about drowning mice and running out into the Square with next to nothing on. What's got into your foolish heads, for pity's sake?'

She stood frowning at the children, who looked shame-faced and did not know what to do next. Alice spread her hands and looked appealingly at her mother. Willie shifted from one bare foot to the other, shaking his head, and Fred stammered, 'It's the mice, Auntie Patty ... We have to g-get them or they'll all be dead. Please, Auntie Patty, please.'

There was such distress in his face that Auntie Patty stopped scolding, and said in a gentler voice, 'You've all got mice on the brain, young Fred, ever since that circus. Now go upstairs and get dressed, all of you. Nobody's going out there in this weather for mice or elephants or anything else. Off with you, now; and Alice, you help Ben before he catches his death of cold.'

Ben had begun to cry again, and the sounds of his sobs brought his father in from the bakehouse. Flushed from the heat of the ovens, his baker's cap askew on his head and flour on his whiskers, Uncle John strode into the kitchen bringing warmth and laughter on his breath. He picked Ben up and rubbed his floury face against the little boy's tear-stained cheeks, looking over Ben's head at the other children standing uncertainly in their nightclothes, and at Auntie Patty's furrowed brow.

'Hey, there. Hey,' he cried. 'What's to do this morning, then? There's plenty of water outside without having it in-doors as well. Now, laddie, now then. What's all the fuss about?'

Ben raised his head from his father's shoulder and wailed mournfully. 'My snow house, my snow house, it's all spoilt and wet and dirty. I want my snow house back. Bring it back, Dad. Can't you bring it back?' His voice broke on a gulping sob. Auntie Patty's face softened into its usual kindly lines, and Uncle John, giving his little son a great warm hug, rubbed his whiskers against his cheeks, leaving traces of flour amongst the tears. A gust of laughter shook him, and his eyes creased with merriment.

'Nay, lad, I can't bring it back, nor the snow neither. Next winter, maybe, when you're grown bigger, we can make another one. But it's thawing now, and there's a great flood fit for old Noah to sail his Ark on, I reckon. Water, water everywhere. Don't fret, Ben. We'll have snow in plenty next year.'

Alice began to dance up and down on her bare toes. 'Dad,' the words tumbled out of her mouth in a flurry of excitement. 'Dad, Ben's Noah's Ark could sail on the water, couldn't it? We could sail it across the Square for him and he'd be happy. You'd like that, wouldn't you, Bennie?'

Willie and Fred looked at Alice with a wild hope dawning in their eyes. She was so full of surprises and resourcefulness that Fred had come to believe implicitly in her ability to find a solution to any problem. 'If only,' he thought, 'if only they could get to the snow house before it had all melted away. If only the mice could get safely into the Ark. If only ...' Willie dived under the table and dragged out Ben's toy box. Ben struggled out of his father's arms, slid down his legs to the ground, and ran across the kitchen with a joyful shout.

'My Noah's Ark,' he cried, and began to pull his toys out of the box, hurling them all over the floor, until he managed to lift out the Noah's Ark that was right at the bottom. 'My Noah's Ark,' he said with satisfaction. 'There it is. My Noah's Ark can go sailing on the water. My pigs and sheep and all the mouses, they can sail on the water, Dad, can't they? Sail it for me, Willie. Can you sail it for me?' He held it hopefully up to his brother, who took it from him and examined it critically underneath.

'It's watertight, I reckon,' he muttered to Fred. 'I bet it'll float all right.'

'So it should do,' laughed Uncle John, taking the Ark from Willie and holding it out of reach above his head. 'I made it myself, didn't I? It will float all right.'

'But it's not going to float anywhere,' said Auntie Patty, 'until you are all dressed and these toys are picked up. Your father's as bad as any of you. My word, just listen to that rain. Up you go now, all of you. Your Dad wants his breakfast.'

She hustled them out of the kitchen and they ran upstairs even faster than they had first come down. Fumbling with buttons and laces they managed to dress themselves in less than five minutes. Willie and Alice between them heaved and pushed Ben into his clothes and Alice washed the floury tearstains from his face. Then they clattered down again in their boots, to find Uncle John dressed like a deep-sea fisherman in oilskins, with a sou'wester on his head and enormous boots on his feet. He was standing by the window with the Noah's Ark in his hands, fixing a tiny pennant to its roof.

'That won't last long in this rain,' he said, 'but it looks pretty. Here she goes, then. You can stay here and watch through the window. Nice day for a sail.' He opened the outer door, letting in the deafening sound of rain. Ben shouted above the noise.

'Wait, Dad, wait. I'll put my pigs in.'

His father shook his head. 'No pigs, lad. Pigs and water don't agree. You might lose them. And there may not be room for pigs, eh, young Fred?' He winked at Fred, and gave him an odd look. To the end of his days Fred was never quite sure how much Uncle John knew, or guessed, about the secrets of the snow house. But nothing was said, and his uncle turned away and carried the Noah's Ark out into the driving rain.

Auntie Patty and the children clustered round the window, staring out into the drowning Square. Uncle John strode through the swirling water that was already ankle-deep, and his boots made great waves as he tramped through the flood. They had expected him to set the Ark afloat just outside the bakehouse, but instead he went on through the downpour until he reached the middle of the Square where the ruined snow house stood. Fred, watching anxiously, saw him stoop over it, walk round it, and examine it closely.

Then he stood up, raised the Ark high above his head for the children to see, and set it down beside the great ball of melting snow. It rocked gently from side to side, but it did not float away. Uncle John stood looking at it for a moment or two, then turned and splashed back to the bakehouse. When he came in, water ran from the brim of his sou'wester and dripped from his oilskins on to the kitchen floor in enormous puddles. Fred wondered whatever Aunt Jen would have said. Auntie Patty simply took Uncle John's wet clothes from him and hung them by the sink to drip into a bucket, and put his slippers on the hearth to warm.

Uncle John mopped his hands and face with a huge towel and smiled at Ben, who was jumping up and down on the hearthrug. 'It's not sailing, Dad. My Noah's Ark's not sailing on the water. It's got stuck.'

His father threw down the towel and lifted Ben up to look out of the window. 'Just wait and see, lad. It will sail all right. It's moored now by your snow house waiting for a crew.' Again he looked across at Fred with a curious expression in his eyes, and Fred looked back at him, uncertain.

'Well,' cried Uncle John with a great laugh breaking out of his mouth, 'there's your Noah's Ark, Ben. Keep your eye on it till you see it floating. It won't go far away, I reckon. There won't be a rainbow, but it might land up on a hilltop ... you never know. And now, if nobody minds, do you think I might have some breakfast?'

[24]

It was midday before the Ark began to move. Fred had his face glued to the window all morning, trying to penetrate the curtain of rain and see what was happening. Ben had long since grown tired of watching and was playing with his wooden animals on the floor, talking to himself. Willie and Alice moved restlessly about the kitchen, playing with Ben and talking to Fred who refused to leave his post at the window. They were all unaccustomed to being housebound, and were at a loss to know what to do with themselves if they could not go freely in and out.

It was Auntie Patty, passing the window on her way to the ovens in the bakehouse with a tray of lardy scones, called 'fat rascals', in her hands ready to be baked for the children's tea, who first noticed the floating of the Ark. 'Look out there,' she said casually. 'I do believe that Noah's Ark's on the move.' Fred had been staring for so long that he did not believe it. He rubbed his eyes and looked again.

It really was happening. Ben's Noah's Ark, its pennant, though bedraggled, still miraculously flying, had taken to the water. Rocking gently, it started to float away from the broken snow house across the flooded Square. Its course

was erratic and ungoverned, but at least it was afloat, moving quietly on the stream. Fred had no means of knowing whether it was an empty craft or a boatful of mice. He could only watch its progress as it tossed about on the swirling waters, and pray for a miracle. Willie and Alice joined him at the kitchen window while he watched the little ship sailing away into the distance. It danced gaily on the surface of the flood, growing smaller and smaller as it went farther away, until at last it was taken out of their sight, round the corner in the direction of The Sundial.

Fred drew a deep breath. The Ark had disappeared. The snow house was destroyed, and only a small grey hillock remained to remind him of its beauty. The magic was gone forever. He turned back from his dream to face the real world of Auntie Patty's dumplings for dinner, and the glowing warmth of the bakehouse fire.

[25]

The sound of drenching rain had not penetrated the thick walls of the snow house until well after dawn, and even when they heard it the mice did not recognize their peril. It was dark and snug inside their fortress, and the feeling of the rapid thaw had not reached them. Even if it had, they would not have understood it. Caradoc himself, with all his ancient wisdom, did not recognize the danger that threatened them. It was not until later in the morning, when trickles of water began to appear round their feet, and large drops fell from the roof on to their furry bodies, that they became alarmed. Then they scampered about in agitation, shaking the water distastefully from their claws. Suddenly a large lump of melting snow fell from one of the windows, and panic seized the company. They ran hither and thither, squeaking piteously, unable to understand what was happening. Several of them tried to escape through the doorway, but when they encountered the flood waters they fled back inside, shrieking with terror. Caradoc attempted to rally them but all his efforts were in vain. Confronted by an incomprehensible horror, the mice gave themselves up for lost. After all their adventures and perilous escapes, this final disaster appeared to be insurmountable. Their last refuge was collapsing about their heads and water was creeping about their feet. Death by drowning seemed inevitable. Their hearts grew faint, and the small supply of courage that was left to them melted away with the melting snow. They clustered together in despair, climbing over each other to escape the rising waters, but they had given up all hope of survival.

'We're done for,' muttered Arthington, and lowering his courageous head to the ground, he closed his eyes and waited for the end.

A piercing squeak reached his ears. He looked up and saw Singleton perched in a window embrasure, dancing like a madman, his whiskers flickering and his tail waving wildly. In the economical shorthand of their own language, information was pouring out of him.

'A house ... a shelter ... up here ... come, come ...'

Arthington did not believe a word of it, but the urgency of Singleton's appeal made him struggle to his feet and in a series of jumps he joined the little mouse at his look-out post. There, rocking gently beside the melting roof of the snow house, a large wooden object floated on the surface of the water. Ben's Noah's Ark, spacious and empty and dry, bumped quietly against the wall.

There was a tiny ladder made of matchwood leading up to its deck, and the hold looked deep and roomy. Arthington ran up the ladder and with sniffing nose and scampering feet made a rapid exploration of the craft. Then he ran down again, and crouching in the window beside Singleton he cried out to the mice below.

'Caradoc, Sir. There's still a chance. Singleton has found a boat out here. It's dry. It floats. It's safe. Come up quickly, come.'

A thrill of hope revived the mice. Led by Caradoc they reached the window in a series of eager leaps, scampered up the ladder one after another and dived into the shelter of the hold. It was too good to be true, thought Almond as he jumped painfully from the window on to the deck. He was the last to leave, and just as he reached the safety of the Ark it began to drift away, tossed like a cork on the water.

It rocked and spun, carried in various directions by the waves. Rain drummed pitilessly on the roof, but the deck was fairly well protected from the downpour, and down below in the hold the mice were quite dry. The curious motion of the Ark made them feel slightly sick, but they were too grateful for its protection to complain. Five of them remained on deck: Caradoc, of course, Arthington, Almond and Singleton, and young Calverley, who would not leave Arthington's side. They crouched together under the shelter of the roof, peering through the rain to see where their floating house was taking them.

The Ark travelled as they did themselves, never in a straight line. It tacked from side to side in its zig-zag progress back along the same route that they had taken when they had first left The Sundial; back across the Square; back to their own real home.

For three days the children did not go to school. The floods rose, and the snow in the streets melted away in muddy rivulets. The rain continued all Wednesday and Thursday, but before dawn on Friday a great wind arose, bringing down chimney-pots and howling through doorways and windows. The rain ceased, and the wind went on blowing until midday on Saturday, drying up the water in the Square until the stone setts were visible once more, broken and cracked by the power of snow and frost.

Auntie Patty looked out of the window. 'What a mercy,' she said. 'It's dried up for your Dad to come home. Watch the window, young Fred. You'll be able to see the smoke from your chimney before long. I'm just going over to The Sundial to light the kitchen fire.'

'It's a pity you've got to go home,' said Alice. 'Couldn't Fred stay here a bit longer, Mam?'

Auntie Patty smiled. 'He's got his own bed to go to and his Dad wants him back,' she replied gently. 'You'll see him tomorrow, I don't doubt.' And she set off to The Sundial, her skirts whipped about her ankles by the gusty wind.

Fred could not see The Sundial from where he was, but after a while he saw a thin grey curl of smoke rising above the roof-tops, and the sight of it made him suddenly long for home and his father and Puss. With a deep sigh he pressed his nose against the window pane, misting it up with his breath. Alice came over to him and put her arm round his shoulder.

'Fire's going,' she said.

'Yes,' said Fred.

'If it's dry tomorrow we might go seeking Ben's Ark, after Chapel,' Alice said. 'It'd be a pity if he lost it.'

Nobody had mentioned the mice since the Ark had floated away on the flood. Fred did not reply. The touch of Alice's hair on his face reminded him so much of his mother that he could not speak. Alice was silent for a moment, and then she said, 'What do you think, young Fred?'

Fred turned to her with a sudden grin. 'I reckon we might,' he said.

*

Fred had expected his father to come and fetch him home, and at six o'clock, when Uncle John came into the kitchen and announced that he was going to take him to The Sundial, disappointment made his mouth drop. 'I thought Dad was coming for me,' he said dolefully. 'Isn't he coming, then? Aunt Jen'll be getting the tea.'

'Your Dad asked me to bring you, lad.' Uncle John's face was a mass of wrinkled smiles. 'They've been home this last half hour, and they can't wait to see you.'

'They'. Fred had a vision of his father sitting in his high-backed chair by the fire, his hat perched on the back of his head, and his pipe, which he hardly ever really smoked, in his hand; and Aunt Jen fussing about at the stove, sniffing in disapproval of the world in general. He sighed as deeply as he had sighed when he was standing at the kitchen window longing for home. Auntie Patty's warm hands were helping him into his coat, and Willie and Alice were jigging about the kitchen, wishing him goodbye as if he were going beyond their ken forever. Ben, however, was more matter of fact.

'You see if my kitten's grown, won't you, Fred? I can have my kitten when it's grown. It can go sailing on the water in my Noah's Ark, can't it, Willie?'

The tense moment broke into laughter. Auntie Patty picked Ben up and swung him round. Uncle John thumped his fist into his hand.

'There . . . bless me, I forgot to tell you. I found your Ark, Ben, high and dry and none the worse for the weather. Stuck on the top of the coal hole in your back yard, young Fred, just by the cellar window. I've brought it home to give it a lick of paint.'

Ben pranced with delight. 'Where is it, Dad? Where's my Noah's Ark?'

'In the shed, lad. I'll paint it up for you tomorrow. Come on, young Fred. Time to go home.' He put on his greatcoat and held out a broad friendly hand, and they went out together into the darkening Square.

Uncle John stopped at the corner. 'You go on now, lad, and I'll be getting back. Tell your Dad I'll be along in the morning. Here's your bag.'

He gave Fred a friendly push. Lights were shining in all the windows of The Sundial, and the bottle-glass panes of the shop-front gleamed and twinkled in the dusk. Fred pressed down the latch and opened the kitchen door, letting out a flood of light. Then he stood stock still in the doorway, clutching his canvas bag, unable to believe his eyes.

She could create chaos out of order in five minutes. There was a cup of tea, half-drunk and left to go cold, on the hearth. Her scarf and gloves were tossed on to the floor beside her chair. Her bag was open on the table, the contents spilling out of it in a drift of sweet-smelling confusion. The entire kitchen was blissfully and comfortably untidy, and all Aunt Jen's regulation and orderliness had disappeared. And it was home again for Fred, sweet, sweet home. For there, sitting by the fire, her face flushing with pleasure, was Mam; and Puss lay purring across her knee.

'Hello, young Fred,' she said. 'What a big lad you've grown. I hardly know you.'

'Mam,' said Fred. 'Oh Mam.'

*

Fred stayed up late that night, listening to his parents' talk, quietly contented. They had not told him, his mother explained to him, about her home-coming in case at the last minute anything went wrong. It was to be a surprise. And Aunt Jen? She was of course party to the secret, and so were Auntie Patty and Uncle John. Aunt Jen would not be coming back. In a week or two she would be looking after some other relations who needed her. Her mission in life was to go from household to household in times of sickness, births and deaths, and she scoured away troubles with her brushes and mops as well as she knew how.

'She does her best, does Jen,' said his father apologetically, and young Fred was too grateful to be free of her compulsive cleansing to say a word.

He did not say a word, either, about the mice, and though he did tell Mam about the snow house Uncle John had made, he could not explain its magic. 'It's gone now,' he said. 'The rain took it away. You never saw it, Mam, and it's melted.' A shadow crossed his face, and his father, seeing the darkness in his eyes, tapped him briskly on the head with the stem of his pipe.

'Time you were in bed, young Fred. Just look at that clock. Whatever would Aunt Jen say?' His voice was full of chuckles, and Fred took his candle and was ready to go upstairs.

'Wait for me,' said Mam, getting up and dislodging Puss from her lap. Puss stretched and yawned, arching her back, and went towards the door that led to the shop and the cellars, looking back at Fred with luminous eyes.

'I'll just let her through,' he murmured. He opened

the door, and together they went out into the dark passage. Puss ran before him towards the cellars. The door at the top of the steps stood ajar, and once more Puss looked back at Fred, inviting him to follow. Softly they went on down the cold steps. The wavering candle flame made the shadows dance on the cobwebby walls, and threw small pools of shifting light on to the dusty floor below. Puss led him on past the flour bins into the farthest cellar. There she stopped, and jumping to the top of an empty wooden box, she sat down and began to wash her paws.

Fred stood very still. Holding his candle high, he whispered into the dark. 'Caradoc ... Almond ... Singleton ... are you there? Are you there, Caradoc?'

Only a faint rustling answered him. It could have been the wind, stirring the papers and cardboard boxes on the floor. Staring through the dusty gloom, Fred thought he caught sight of a whisking tail, and could hear a pattering of tiny paws and an occasional squeak. Puss jumped on to his shoulder, rubbing her head under his chin and purring loudly in his ear. Her golden eyes gazed into his, and she uttered a little crow. Then she leapt to the ground and danced lightly up the cellar steps, a small black shadow in the darkness of the night. She disappeared through the doorway. She had her own appointments to keep – and Fred knew that the mice had come home.

His mother's voice called down from the kitchen. 'Are you coming, young Fred?'

Carrying his flickering candle he climbed slowly up the stone stairs. At the top he turned, and whispered, 'Good night, Caradoc.' Then he went back into the bright warmth of the kitchen, where his mother was waiting to take him to bed.

'Everything's all right,' he thought contentedly to himself as he lay in bed in the dark. 'Everything's all right now Mam's come home.' He pushed his hand under his pillow, and for a moment he imagined he touched the soft fur of a baby mouse, and felt the cold prick of a tiny claw on his hand. But it was only the little wooden mouse his father had made him. His fingers closed lovingly round it, and he fell asleep.